THE TALL STRANGER

A NOVEL

O. L. BROWN

The Tall Stranger

Unless otherwise noted, all scripture quotations are taken from the King James Version (KJV) Bible.

Cover Design by Ian Schrauth, Starboat, LLC

This book is published by the author and Kindle Direct Publishing

Comments and questions are welcome and may be forwarded to the author at:
obrown281@aol.com

2nd Edition 05/23

3rd Edition 07/23

SCRIPTURE

Whoso findeth a wife findeth a good thing, and obtaineth favor of the Lord.

Proverbs 18: 22

ACKNOWLEDGMENT

A special thanks to Deanna Lucas for reviewing the manuscript of this book and suggesting revisions and improvements.

ADDITIONAL COMMENTS

This book is a work of fiction, however the meetings at the Bunch of Grapes Tavern, the formation of the Ohio Company, and the awarding of land in the Ohio Territory are historically correct. Also, Grace Gowden Galloway is an actual historical Loyalist who supported the King, and who lost her and her husband's property, until it was restored to her after the war.

Books by O. L. Brown

<u>Fiction</u>

Northern Lights
Sappa Creek Road
The Prairie Wind
Shadows of the Past
The Man from Wyoming
Superstition Mountain Dreams
The Letter
The Cabin
The Tall Stranger
Roman Holiday
The Stars Look Down
Into the Rising Dawn

<u>Non-Fiction</u>

Twelve Little Known People of the Bible
Christianity and the Wealth of Nations
Seven Bible Characters

O. L. Brown

The
TALL
STRANGER

CHAPTER 1

Tall Man Riding

An early spring sun, losing some of its earlier warmth, was dropping low in the west over the Blue Mountains. A purple haze had begun to thicken in the timbered notches and the long, sweeping gray round and billowing hills. Splotches of red and yellow flowers, which lay thick along the hillsides, caught the waning sunlight and brought a brief smile to the face of the tall man. Through the distant haze he could see the reflection of the sunlight on the snow that still lingered along the high ridges of the mountains.

The man rode astride a dark gray, almost black horse, with a flowing mane, and three white legs that anyone knowledgeable of horse flesh would discern as being a cut or two above the average horse seen along the frontier, west of the Allegheny Mountains. When the man rode the horse through a town or settlement, those who knew fine horseflesh usually halted in mid step and would remark on the quality and beauty of the animal. A large, mixed, collie-shepherd dog trotted beside the horse, the end of its tongue protruding from the side of its mouth. Behind the horse and dog, a heavily laden burro plodded along, its head down in apparent indifference to the man, the horse, or dog.

He directed the horse away from the heavily timbered hillside, passed along the slope of the hill, and began a descent towards the river and the cluster of buildings that lay below him. The settlement of Sumerill's Ferry lay hard against a bend of the

Youghiogheny River, a few miles from where it flowed into the Monongahela River and some thirty miles southeast of Pittsburgh, Pennsylvania. Across the river, a heavily timbered hill rose up above the settlement, sheltering it from the north.

As he rode down the hillside and neared the river, his alert eyes took in the rough buildings of log cabins, and huts of the frontier settlement that lay scattered, in a haphazard fashion, along the banks of the river. His first impression was that he might have difficulty finding a room where he could shelter from the incessant rain that seemed to come during each night. He had been traveling for nearly a month and he, and his horse and burro, were tired and worn and he would welcome the possibility of a good night's rest under a roof and sheltered from the rain and wind.

The man's name was Jean LaBerge, lately from Middlebury, Vermont. He was a tall, lithe man, with broad, muscular shoulders, and strong arms and legs that were clad in buckskin breeches and shirt. A tricorne, or "cocked hat" sat lightly atop his full head of black hair. A pistol was tucked behind his belt, a bowie knife was strapped to his side, and a long rifle lay in a scabbard alongside the saddle.

It was early in the spring of 1784, as Jean LaBerge rode his horse into the settlement of Sumerill's Ferry. As he neared the edge of the settlement, he drew his horse and burro to a stop and let his eyes roam over the scattered log cabins and rough buildings that had been thrown up along the banks of the river. He directed his attention along the street of the settlement. The recent rains had turned the street into a sea of muddy wagon ruts and water filled holes. About halfway along the street, he espied a hand painted sign that advertised the *BURNHAM TAVERN*. Many of these frontier taverns had rooms to let for the night, although many offered only a back room, where several beds were laid out side by side. He wasn't keen on sharing a room with others, but he'd take a look at the accommodations, if any were available. At worst, he would enjoy a pint of ale before further effort to locate a place to shelter for the night. He touched his heels lightly to his horse, and the horse, burro, and dog moved on along the muddy street toward the sign.

8

He drew his animals to a halt near the corner of the tavern and surveyed the ankle-deep mud and water, which lay along the street, with some distaste. He glanced about and espied a slightly raised spot along the side of the building, which seemed to be mostly free of mud and water. He guided his horse and burro to this higher ground and dismounted. There was no post or rail to tether his animals, however, a cart lay up against the side of the building and he quickly tied the horse and burro to the cart. He looked down at the dog as he said, "Stay here Shag. Don't let anyone mess with the horse or burro." He stooped and patted the dog lightly on the head, as the dog wagged its tail. He turned and trying to avoid the worst of the mud, he made his way around to the front of the building and the boardwalk.

Due to his six-foot, two-inch height, he found it necessary to duck his head as he entered the log building. Once inside he stopped and took in the dim scene. Several rough, hand-made tables and chairs were scattered about a small room, and a rough wood counter ran along the side of the room. The floor was rough planking and covered with sawdust, as well as a good accumulation of dirt. A heavy stone fireplace filled the far wall, although no fire was in evidence.

Two men were seated at a table, their buckskins rough and dirty. They were each nursing a pint of ale they held cupped in their hands. The two men glanced up at him but offered no greeting. LaBerge eyed the men for a moment and then turned to the log counter.

A short, heavily whiskered man stood behind the counter with a dirty apron wrapped about his waist. LaBerge approached the counter and spoke in his deep timbered voice. "I'd appreciate a glass of ale. I'm right dry!"

The whiskered bartender looked at him for a moment, obviously sizing up a stranger, and then said, "Sure thing. I'll have it for ya in a jiffy."

LaBerge watched as the man shuffled to the end of the counter, took down a glass from a shelf, and then slid it under the spigot of a dark and heavy oak barrel that stood at the end of the counter and against the far wall. Within moments the glass was full of dark brown ale. The whiskered man returned along the counter and set the glass down in front of LaBerge. "Here ya are mister. That'll be two bits."

LaBerge opened the leather pouch that was tied to his waist, took out the correct change and laid it on the counter. He took a long draw of the drink, looked about the room for a moment and then said, "Do you have any beds for the night?"

The whiskered man looked across the counter at him for a long moment before replying, "Sorry mister, we only have four beds set up in the back room, and they're all spoken for."

"I'm sorry to hear that, but I'll make do."

The whiskered man studied LaBerge again for a long moment and then said, "Yer a stranger hereabouts. Where ya from?"

"Vermont," LaBerge replied. "A right good ride from here."

"The bartender grinned at him through his whiskers. "Yeah, ya been a travelin' a far piece! You travelin' lonesome or with a party?"

"Just my horse, burro and dog; no one else. I left the horse and burro tied to the wagon alongside the tavern. There's less mud there. Hope you don't mind?"

"No, not at all." The whiskered man fell silent for a moment and then said, "I bet ya is headed to some of that new country we just got from them Englishers at the end of the war, when we signed the treaty in Paris. Are ya headed for the Ohio Territory?"

"Yes, as a veteran of the war of independence, I've been awarded rights to prove up a plot of land. I'm going to a place that some call the Blue Valley." LaBerge paused for only a moment. He wasn't interested in giving this man a detailed report on either his past or his future plans. He quickly changed the subject as he said,

"Do you know when the next flatboat leaves downriver for Pittsburg? My horse and burro are worn down some and I'd like to take the boat and give them a rest."

The whiskered man grinned at LaBerge as he said, "Seems like there's lots of folks headed west to the wild frontier these days, since we signed the treaty with the British and put an end ta the war." The whiskered face looked up at LaBerge as he continued, "Sure, ya can catch the boat to Pittsburgh. In fact, they just put on another boat. I think there's one leaves here early tomorrow morning. You just head on down ta the river and ya will see the boat shack. Ya can book passage there for yourself and yer animals."

"Thanks," he replied. "I'll do that." He downed the last of his ale and started to turn and then stopped. "Is there a stable here, were. I can hay and grain my animals and a man might sleep for the night?"

The fat man pointed on down the street. "Putnam's Livery," he said. "Just head on down the street and ya can't miss it. Putnam will most likely let ya sleep somewhere in the shed where ya can stable and feed yer horses. He won't charge ya extra if you stable yer horse there."

"Thanks mister." LaBerge turned and glanced about the room. He noticed that the two men had left, their empty ale bottles sitting on the table. He looked back at the whiskered man. "If I come back in an hour, can you rustle me something to eat." He rubbed the front of his shirt. "I feel like I could chew up a good bit of a bear!"

"Sure can! The missis will stuff ya with some venison, potatoes, an' gravy."

"I'm much obliged. I'll see you in an hour." LaBerge nodded at the man, went to the entrance, and ducked his head as he stepped through the door.

He paused and glanced to the west to see a blood red sun hanging just above the hills, its brilliance muted in the blue haze that hung across the mountains. The imminent setting of the sun made him realize that he was tired and worn. He hoped he could find a dry place to spend the night. He made his way along the dirty boardwalk, which fronted the tavern, and as he neared the corner of the building leading to the alley, he was startled to hear the low growl of his dog.

He stopped and quickly looked around the corner of the tavern and along the alley. His dog was crouched near the middle of the alley, his teeth bared, as low growls came from his throat. He could see nothing amiss as he stepped forward into the alley. He directed his attention to the dog as he said, "What is it boy? What's the matter?"

As he spoke to the dog, he was startled to see the heads of two men rise above the far side of the cart. He immediately recognized them as the two men that had been drinking ale at the table in the tavern.

Each man held a pistol that was leveled across the cart at him. One of the men spoke in a hard voice, "Put yer hands up mister. Were gonna clean ya out. Looks like ya got a good bit of nice stuff here in yer burro's pack and we'll take yer coin pouch and yer guns as well. We heard ya talkin' ta the fat man in the tavern. Ha! Ha!"

LaBerge said nothing as he stared across the cart at the two men. The ominous silence that filled the narrow alley was broken only by the low growl of the dog. and then the second man spoke. "Get a move on mister! Get them hands up high!"

These two men didn't realize it, but they had made three mistakes. They had misjudged the character of the tall man and his likely response to their demands; they had dismissed the dog as an animal with a growl and nothing more; and they had unwittingly placed themselves in a vulnerable position on the far side of the cart. The cart was relatively small and empty and as LaBerge stepped to the edge of the cart he spoke in a calm voice, "Ya got me, but can we make a deal. I need to keep my long rifle and a few things. Ya can't just clean me out!"

"No deals mister," cried the first man, "We got ya over a barrel! You get yer hands up and ----"

LaBerge's next move was swift and powerful as he grasped the bed of the cart and heaved it up and into the two men, sending the men sprawling back into the mud. As he heaved the cart up, he yelled. "Get 'em Shag!"

The two men had lost their pistols when they were knocked to the ground when the cart slammed into them. They were struggling to regain their footing when the dog hit them with all of his forty pounds, his mouth wide open in snarling rage. It seemed that he was everywhere. His initial rush sent one man sprawling back down into the mud and he then immediately turned on the other man as he struggled to rise from the mud, sinking his teeth into the man's leg just above the knee. The man screamed in pain as he attempted to shake off the dog.

LaBerge was around the cart in a moment, and he swiftly grabbed the first man and hit him hard across the face, sending blood gushing from his nose and lips. As the man fell back into the mud LaBerge yelled, "Stay down or I'll give ya more!"

Shag held the second man's leg in his mouth with a firm grip as the man cursed and tried to shake off the dog. LaBerge swung hard with a heavy right fist that caught the man on the side of his face, sending him smashing into the wall of the tavern where he lay groaning in pain. He made no attempt to rise.

LaBerge swiftly retrieved the men's pistols from the mud, and then said, "Get up. There must be a lawman here in this settlement and I'm going to see that you get acquainted with him."

He marched the two men from the alley and back into the tavern, the dog followed, his teeth barred and growling. The fat tavernkeeper looked up as they stepped through the door, surprise across his face. He said nothing for a moment as he surveyed the men's bloody faces and torn shirts. "Looks as if ya have had a run-in with these two scallywags. I thought I heard something from outside but didn't give it much thought."

LaBerge shoved the men forward as he said, "They were waiting for me in the alley and planned to take my money, and goods.

13

What have you got for law hereabouts? I'd like to see these men locked up."

"The fat man smiled at LaBerge as he said, "Yeah, we got a sheriff and a jail of sorts. I'll send my boy to fetch him."

An hour later LaBerge had sworn out a complaint against the two men and they were seated in a make-shift jail in a dark log building. The sheriff had said, "The circuit judge will be by in a week, or so, and I'll let him see your complaint and he can then hand down sentence on the men." He had smiled at LaBerge, then continued, "I see that you and your dog didn't have much trouble handling these two men." He let his eyes run across LaBerge. "I'd guess ya have been around the horn and up the creek a few times."

LaBerge's face carried a dead pan look as he replied to the sheriff, "Yeah, I'm just a hard rock farm boy from Vermont who has needed to tackle a few hard rocks along the way."

CHAPTER 2

The Tall Stranger

Jean LaBerge kicked the straw the stableman had thrown down into the stall, up into a pile and then smoothed it out to a six-inch deep bed He found his blanket in the pack he had removed from the burro and spread it out over the straw. He turned back to the pack and dug out his bearskin coat and threw the heavy coat down at the edge of the blanket. This would be his bed tonight. He'd slept in worse.

He'd returned to the tavern and taken the hearty meal the tavern keeper's wife had prepared for him and then booked passage for himself and his horse and burro on the flatboat that left for Pittsburg at eight tomorrow morning. The man at the ticket shack had told him that it usually took about ten hours to make the journey downriver to Pittsburg. The ticket agent had looked up at LaBerge as he said, "The boat's tied up at the dock now, so feel free ta look her over if ya like."

LaBerge wasn't sure how well his horse and burro would take to the riverboat ride. He'd never ridden one of the strange looking contraptions himself, however, he was by nature and upbringing an inquisitive man and he was looking forward to the experience of riding the riverboat to the Ohio and then on down the Ohio River until he reached Huntington at the northeast edge of Kentucky. When he left the flatboat at Huntington, he'd resume riding his horse northeast into the Ohio wilderness until he reached his property in what some called the Blue Valley.

He'd spent several minutes looking over the long flat-bottomed boat that was tied up alongside the plank dock at the river's edge. He walked along the wharf as he surveyed the approximately sixty-foot length of the flatboat and smiled to himself. It struck him that the craft was best described as a mixture of log cabin, floating barnyard, and country grocery store. The rear third of the boat was open and floored with heavy oak planking. Sawdust and straw were spread ankle deep across the planks. This was the "barnyard" for the horses, cattle, and wagons that were riding the riverboat. A hitching rail had been constructed along the front of the barnyard. He smiled to himself as he wondered how long it would take for his horse and burro to get their "sea legs." In front of the barnyard the combination cabin and store took most of the remainder of the front half of the boat, except for an eight-foot open space along the front railing where passengers could loiter and smoke as the boat moved along the river.

When he looked to the roof of the cabin, he saw a nearly forty-foot boom, or pole, that lay in a large wooden swivel atop the cabin and ran back beyond the rear of the flatboat to a six-foot long rudder. He'd guessed it would take two strong men to handle the rudder, especially in rough water. He'd get a chance to inspect the cabin tomorrow when he boarded, however when he looked through a window, he could make out several small tables, chairs, and benches, and what appeared to be a small store that sold food items to the travelers. Small rowboats were strapped to each side of the flatboat.

The liveryman, who owned the stable, had readily granted his request to sleep in the stable. The man had hitched up his pants as he said, "Sure, ya can sleep here with yer animals. I'll throw down a mite of straw for ya ta sleep on."

His horse and burro were stabled a few feet away from his straw bed, where they munched contentedly on a liberal quantity of grain and hay. He'd told the liveryman, "Give the horse and burro an

16

extra portion; we've come a good piece and they've earned it over the past few weeks."

He sat down on the blanket, pulled off his moccasins and shirt, and pulled the bear coat up over his waist, with his arms laying atop the coat. Within a few minutes his eyes were closed, and the tall man from Vermont was sleeping soundly.

Jean LaBerge had been born and raised on a Vermont farm. He had known much hard work and hardship, great sorrow and seemingly insurmountable obstacles most of his life. It was what was to be expected, just as one was expected to measure up. He was young at twenty-four, but even at that youthful age he had seen much, done much, and survived much. During those few years he'd been "up the creek and around the horn" as the saying went. His parents had been strict and firm in their upbringing of their only son and he had been taught the value of hard work, integrity, and kindness. The tall man from Vermont was full of wisdom and an understanding of human nature well beyond his seemingly few years of age.

When the Revolutionary War had come, he had immediately joined the Green Mountain Boys, a Vermont militia organized by Ethan Allen in the late 1760's to resist New York's attempts to control all of New England. He had joined the militia out of some patriotism, but mostly it had been a way of escape from the hard, rocky land where he had grown to become a man. He carried a twinge of guilt that he had abandoned the farm to his parents during those long years of the war. He had been with the Green Mountain Boys when Ethan Allen had led them in capturing Fort Ticonderoga on Lake Champlain. As the war had dragged on, he had endured the snow, the cold, the privations, and freezing nights of Valley Forge, with General George Washington in command. He'd fought British soldiers at the bloody battles of Kings Mountain and Cowpens and had been present when Cornwallis had surrendered the British troops at Yorktown. Over the course of those long hard years of war, his dedication, hard work, and attention to detail had enabled him to rise through the ranks until he had been made a Major in the Continental Army.

When the war had finally ground to an end, he had left the army and returned home to find his mother resting in the patch of ground that served as a cemetery behind the small, white steepled church that stood at the edge of the small town a few miles from the farm. In addition, he had found his father worn, tired and aged beyond his years.

His father, Rufus LaBerge, a good and proud man had, in the long family tradition pursued a life of tilling the rocky Vermont soil, where he had eked out a hard scrabble living that put sufficient food on the table to avoid starvation, but little else. Jean had returned to farming as he helped his father gather in the meager crops that fall. The winter had been long, cold, and wet, even when measured against the usual Vermont winters, and his father had heeded the "call of the Lord" before the frost had left the ground as spring had come on, and he now lay beside LaBerge's mother in the church cemetery.

As a result of his distinctive service as an officer in the Continental Army during the war, he had been invited to come to Boston and meet with a group of ten men at the Bunch of Grapes Tavern located at the corner of King and Kilby Streets. The purpose of the group was to launch a highly ambitious plan to acquire land in the immense reach of the unsettled wilderness known as the Northwest Territory that had been ceded to the United States at the Paris Peace Treaty that had brought an end to hostilities between England and the United States.

This new land, was spoken of as "the back country," or simply as the "howling wilderness." It was the land beyond the Ohio River; that great highway west; *la Belle Riviere,* as the early French Explorer Rene-Robert Cavalier Sieur de La Salle had called it. There were no roads, no bridges, and only a few scattered settlements in this vast, unexplored wilderness. The few people that had made their way west into this unexplored wilderness were mostly hunters, trappers, fur traders, and squatters, who settled wherever they chose and without legal claim to the land. In addition, men who were wanted by the law for various crimes of murder and robbery, had fled west to become "lost" in this vast, unending wilderness, where there was no law to bring them to justice. The reports were that this was forest land teaming with deer, elk, wolves, bears, wild boars, panthers, rattlesnakes, and Indians.

The war was over, his father was dead, and Jean LaBerge was on his way to claim a piece of this wilderness land that was being made available to veterans of the war, at a bargain price, as compensation for their services during the war of independence.

To Jean LaBerge the "howling wilderness" of the west beyond the Ohio River was his future, and shortly after his father's death he had sold the rocky farm and traveled to the meeting at the Bunches of Grapes tavern in Boston. When he had left the final meeting at the tavern, the Ohio Company had been formed and he had been granted three shares in the newly organized land venture. Three shares represented a grant of 1,200 acres of land of his choosing in the "howling wilderness" west of the Ohio River. He carried a rough map that had been prepared by a trapper and hunter who had recently returned from the western wilderness. "It's a lovely valley," he had exclaimed as he handed the sketch to LaBerge. "As ya can see, I've called it the 'Blue Valley.' The soil is rich, and the hills are full of deer and bear. What more could a man ask for?" He had grinned up at LaBerge as he exclaimed, "Ya need to get herself a sturdy woman and go west to the Blue Valley."

He had left almost immediately. His few affairs had been quickly put in order and his meager belongings packed onto the back of the burro. He had left Vermont and traveled steadily west, sleeping in the open when the weather was agreeable and staying a few nights in taverns to avoid the worst of the rain. The first formidable barrier to his progress had been the Allegheny Mountains, where his travel had been slow and arduous through the rain, sleet, and occasional snow squall, as he had made his way through these rugged mountains.

From time to time, he had joined with other men and families that were also on their way to Kentucky and the Northwest Territory. He, and his traveling companions had crossed the Tuscarora Mountain, slogging through rain, heavy mists and cold winds. The cold damp nights were spent around huge, blazing fires as many of his traveling companions imbibed liberal quantities of whiskey to lessen the discomforts. They had finally reached the westernmost edge of the Alleghenies—Laurel Mountain and Chestnut Ridge—but the rains had not ceased. He had left his few traveling companions and had pushed on alone and had now reached Sumerill's Ferry, where tomorrow he would board the flatboat which would carry him west to the Ohio River and the howling wilderness.

CHAPTER 3

The Flatboat

To a tired man the straw and blanket proved to be a comfortable bed and he was grateful for the shelter of the stable against the intermittent rains that swept through during the night. He slept well and was up at six, as the light of a new day began filling the stable.

He pulled on an old pair of work shoes, left over from the farm. It was better to get the shoes muddy than the moccasins. Using an old rag, he'd found lying in the stall, he cleaned yesterday's mud from the moccasins and then stowed them in the burro's pack. He stepped outside the entrance to the stable to a barrel of rainwater, washed his hands, arms and face, and slicked down his hair. He returned inside and dipped out a small quantity of grain from a wooden box and spread it out in the trough, and then forked down some hay for his horse and burro.

He turned to the dog that followed along behind him, observing his every move. "Stay here Shag and watch the horses and pack. I'll be back as soon as I've rustled up something to eat. I'll bring something for you when I return."

As he walked to the tavern, he was pleased to see patches of blue appearing in the morning sky as the night's rainclouds moved east, and dissipated, heralding a mostly sunny day. He ducked into the tavern and was directed by the tavern keeper to a seat at a table near the front window. When he ordered his breakfast, he said to the whiskered man. "If your wife can spare some scraps of meat for my dog it will be appreciated."

"Sure thing," grinned the innkeeper. "I'll have the missis fix up a sack of scraps for him."

"Thanks. Add a bit to my bill to cover the food for the dog."

As he waited for his breakfast, LaBerge took in the activity outside the tavern window. Two wheeled carts and four wheeled wagons, pulled by oxen, mules, and horses moved in both directions along the wet and muddy street. Occasionally, he heard the snap of a whip or the loud oath of a driver as he urged his animals along. It was early morning but many men, boys, and a few women were about and moving along the boardwalks that had been constructed along the front of many of the business establishments. LaBerge could see that these boardwalks were much favored by the women who walked along the walkways with their long skirts held up a couple of inches to avoid trailing in the mud that had been deposited by the traffic along the walkways.

Within a few minutes the innkeeper returned with a tray bearing his breakfast and he immediately fell to eating with a hungry gusto. He was unsure what eating fare would be available on the flatboat.

When he paid for his breakfast, the owner handed him a small sack. "Here's some meat an' scraps for yer dog. I'll bet he'll be pleased."

"Thanks. I'm much obliged and the dog will be mighty happy."

He returned to the stable. As the dog wolfed down the scraps with much wagging of his tail, LaBerge saddled his horse, repacked the pack and tied it onto his burro. He led the horse and burro from the shack, mounted the horse and rode to the river.

When he arrived at the wharf, he continued to sit in his saddle, as he surveyed the waterfront and flatboat in the early morning sun that danced along the flowing river. A beehive of activity stirred all about him as carts and wagons passed or stopped to unload passengers and luggage. Horses, and a few cows, mules and donkeys were being led, pulled, and pushed aboard the flatboat, some fighting back against boarding the strange and unfamiliar contraption. The air was filled with orders being shouted, loud oaths, and hearty greetings.

LaBerge left his saddle and joined this throng of humanity and animals and within an hour he had his horse and burro aboard the flatboat and tied to the hitching rail, where they fed with some contentment on hay that LaBerge had forked from a rack. He had removed the saddle from his horse and the pack from the burro and stowed them, and his long rifle, in a large box that ran along the side of the boat.

Yesterday, when he had walked along the wharf, he had taken note of the name, *The Mayflower,* painted in bold letters across the flatboat's low stern. LaBerge was of the opinion that it was an apt name, given the fact that it was to carry him into the unknown, howling wilderness of the Ohio Territory.

He left his horse and burro and took a position along the side of the boat, where he could watch as passengers and animals continued to board the boat. Over the next hour a few more people and animals came aboard the flatboat and then at nine o'clock the heavy ropes that held the boat to the dock were cast free and the flatboat was pushed out into the current of the river. LaBerge looked up to the roof of the cabin and watched two men as they labored to push the large boom back and forth to maneuver the boat out into the river. He loitered at the front of the flatboat for a few minutes and then drifted back to the rear, his dog trotting along at his side, to check on his horse and burro. He was pleased to see that both animals continued to munch on the hay and were unconcerned with the movement of the boat along the river.

He returned to the bow of the boat and leaned against the rail, as he took in the scene that slowly moved past the boat. The passing hills and small mountains lay green and wet, silent and brooding, with the remnants of last night's rain glistening from the leaves of

23

the trees. Most of the rain clouds had now fled east and the morning sun shone, bright and crisp, across the heavily forested hillsides. He shifted his gaze from the hills and down to the river and watched as the blunt bow of the flatboat pushed through the muddy water, sending up a heavy spray. The muddy brown of the moving river was in sharp contrast to the green that rose from its banks and marched up into the far hills. On the far shore, LaBerge espied a buck deer, its head held high, its velvet antlers shining with last night's rain as it watched the flatboat float past.

LaBerge continued to stand at the rail, as the flatboat moved northwest along the river. A few hours passed and they came to the point, at McKeesport, where the Youghiogheny River merged with the larger, muddy yellow, Monongahela. A fellow passenger who stood nearby looked at him as he said, "We've got another twenty miles and we'll be in Pittsburgh and the Ohio River."

LaBerge acknowledged the man's statement by saying, "Yeah, I'll be right pleased to make it to Pittsburg. That brings me much closer to my destination in the Ohio Wilderness."

The sun lay low just above the sharp hills when the boatmen eased the flatboat against the dock in Pittsburgh. LaBerge stood near his horse and burro as they docked. He wanted to make sure the animals didn't become excited during the hustle and bustle of docking.

He looked out across the crude frontier settlement that abutted the river and could see a large scattering of log cabins and a few houses, all built without apparent plan, or organization, along the riverbank and back into the hills. Near the edge of the village, he could see old Fort Pitt. He had overhead one of the passenger's remarks that the fort was inhabited with a "lazy set of beings" where the drinking and export of whisky was its chief business.

Notwithstanding its rough appearance, Pittsburg occupied a key position at the headwaters of the Ohio River and was the gateway to the howling wilderness to the west. Springtime, with the water level high, was the best time to travel the river. LaBerge's heart jumped, and a smile creased his face; he had made it across the formidable Allegheny's and was now at the Ohio River, the jumping off place for those traveling west to the new frontier. What were the challenges and adventures that awaited him in this new land beyond the Ohio River? What would he find when he finally arrived in Blue Valley? How long would it take him to reach his destination?

CHAPTER 4

Hannah Cody

Flatboat travelers, and their animals, were free to spend the night aboard the flatboat, although the boat offered little in the way of sleeping accommodations. The cabin held two very small sleeping rooms and a few cots could be rented and set up about the boat, affording little privacy. LaBerge felt it desirable to give his horse and burro a break from the boat and to give them some exercise. Leaving the pack and saddle in the storage box aboard the boat, he took his animals ashore and sought out a livery where they could spend the night. He purchased an evening meal at a tavern and then returned to the boat and retrieved the blanket, bear coat, and his long rifle. He sought out the captain of the boat, who assured him that his belongings would be safe while he was ashore through the night. "I have an armed guard on duty through the night. He'll see to it your stuff remains safe in the storage box."

However, in view of what had happened in Sumerill's Ferry he was reluctant to leave his long rifle in the storage box overnight. He returned to the stable and purchased some grain and hay for the horse and burro and then bedded down for the night in a corner of the stable.

He was up before sunrise the following morning and had his animals aboard the flatboat and tied to the hitching rail as the sun made its appearance over the eastern hills, its brilliant rays dancing across the river. It hadn't rained during the night and LaBerge viewed the deep blue sky as a good omen as he resumed his journey into the wild frontier. He stowed his blanket and coat back into the storage box and taking his rifle in hand he returned to the tavern and ate a hearty breakfast. When he returned to the boat, he stowed the rifle back into the box and then took a position along the rail to watch as new passengers began boarding the flatboat.

He watched a variety of men, and a few women, scramble up the gangplank and board the boat. A few had animals: mostly horses, which were led up a separate gangplank at the rear of the boat. He was about to leave his place at the rail when his attention was drawn to a team of oxen, pulling a small wagon, as it drew up near the rear gangplank. The driver brought the wagon to a halt and a woman and a young lady of about eighteen alighted from the wagon and stood aside, watching, as the man urged the oxen forward onto the gangplank. Apparently, the gangplank was a new and frightening experience to the oxen, and they stood immobile, refusing to step forward onto the contraption. The driver of the wagon snapped his whip at the animals, urging them forward, but the two beasts continued to stand, immobile, their heads low and swinging from side to side in apparent confusion and fear of the river flowing below the gangplank.

LaBerge observed the oxen and wagon with amusement for a few minutes and then, seeing that the man was having little success in getting the oxen to move forward, he quickly made his way along the rail to the rear gangplank and walked down to the oxen. He looked over the heads of the oxen at the driver as he said, "I'll see if I can help."

He grasped the bridles of each ox and tugged them forward as he spoke to them in soothing tones. "Come on, old boys, you can do it," he intoned.

Apparently, his voice and urgings were a calming influence on the oxen and with halting steps, the two animals began moving up the gangplank and within a few minutes they had pulled the wagon up onto the flatboat. When they were aboard, the driver jumped down and extended his hand to LaBerge's as he said, "I'm much obliged for your help mister." He paused for a moment as if reluctant to ask for more assistance and then he continued, "Would you be so kind as to assist me in unhitching the oxen and maneuvering the wagon into the corner at the rear of the boat? It's sort of a two-man job to move the wagon by hand."

"Sure, that's no problem," replied LaBerge. "I'll be happy to be of assistance." Within a few minutes the oxen had been unhitched from the wagon, tied at the hitching rail, and the wagon had been maneuvered into the back corner of the boat. Before they left the wagon, the man retrieved a small satchel which he carried in his hand as they turned to leave. He offered no explanation as to what the satchel contained. LaBerge suspected that it contained their life savings. He smiled to himself as he patted his own money belt that was strapped beneath his shirt.

The man turned to LaBerge as he said, "I'm Jedidiah Cody and I sure appreciate your assistance. I doubt I could have gotten the oxen and wagon aboard without your help."

LaBerge took the offered hand as he said, "I'm Jean LaBerge. I'm pleased that I could be of some assistance."

Cody turned and looked down at his wife and daughter, who were looking up at them from the wharf. "That's my wife, Cathedra, and my daughter, Hannah." He motioned for the two women to come to the front of the boat as he called out. "Come to the front gangplank and come aboard. I want you to meet this young man who assisted me in getting the wagon and oxen aboard."

LaBerge and Cody made their way forward and met the two women at the top of the gangplank. Cody introduced the two ladies to LaBerge. "Ma, Hannah, this is Jean LaBerge. You need to thank him for his assistance in getting the oxen and wagon aboard the flatboat."

Mrs. Cody extended her hand as she said, "Thank you, Mr. LaBerge. It was very thoughtful of you to lend my husband some assistance."

Hannah drew in her breath as she smiled up at Jean LaBerge. How tall he was! And his broad shoulders seemed to speak of strength and power. She had to fumble for words as she said, "Thank you, Mr. LaBerge, for helping my father with the oxen and wagon. It was very kind of you to come to our assistance."

Jean LaBerge looked down on the young lady who continued to gaze up at him with shining eyes that were shadowed by a large brown bonnet. A tan shawl lay across her shoulders above a scarlet dress that fell below her ankles. He was immediately taken with the shy beauty of her smile.

Jean bowed slightly as he said, "It was my pleasure ma'am." LaBerge motioned toward the front of the flatboat as he glanced at Mr. Cody. "Come, let's find seating for you in the cabin before it fills up."

Within a few moments they were seated at a small corner table near a window which afforded a view forward. "This will do very nicely," exclaimed Mrs. Cody." She turned to her husband, "Jedidiah we must provide this young man with some refreshments in thanks for his assistance."

"Yes, indeed," replied her husband.

He turned to Jean. "I'm not sure what they offer here in the way of refreshments, but what is your preference?"

"I'll drink what you and the lady's drink."

Jedidiah rose from his chair and went to the counter and soon returned with four bottles of a colored drink. "I'm not sure what we have here, but I was assured that it was non-alcoholic."

Within a few minutes the flatboat had cast off from the wharf and began to make its way out into the Ohio River. "Oh, this is exciting!" exclaimed Hannah. "I've never been on a flatboat before."

As the boat moved out into the wide Ohio River Hannah looked across the table at her parents. "Let's go outside and find a place along the rail so we can see everything as we move along the river."

Jedidiah cast a quick glance at Jean as he said, "You have my permission to accompany our daughter outside. My wife and I will keep the table while you're gone. Take your time."

Hannah turned to LaBerge with soft and pleading eyes as she exclaimed. "Oh yes, please accompany me outside and tell me all about everything."

It had been less than an hour since they had met, but Jean LaBerge had become smitten by this beautiful young lady, and he jumped at the opportunity to spend more time with her, even if there were other passengers nearby. He quickly stood to his feet and helped her from her chair. He glanced at her father as he said, "It will be my pleasure sir. I'll see that no harm comes to her."

He took her arm, and they left the cabin and soon found a position at the rail that ran along the bow of the boat. "Oh, this is lovely," she exclaimed as she looked up at him, "Thank you for agreeing to accompany me outside. My father would never have let me come out here alone."

For a moment LaBerge was left tongue-tied as he looked down into the beauty of her sparkling eyes, "It's my pleasure ma'am."

She turned and let her eyes roam ahead of the riverboat and then from shore to shore as they moved along the broad river. LaBerge could hardly take his eyes from her as he watched the soft breeze tug at her bonnet and stir the long, dark curls that hung from the edge of the bonnet. A crazy and sudden thought rattled through his mind; *It would be wonderful if she would accompany him to Blue Valley and become his wife!* He pushed such foolish thoughts from his mind and turned to look at the river ahead. He said nothing as the boat passed by the green, tree-covered hills and small mountains that rose up on both sides of the river. A few minutes later they drifted past a small settlement that lay at the river's edge and watched as a man and a boy waved from the shore.

As they drifted along the river, she said very little, except to comment on the beauty of the rolling green hills or the birds that shadowed the boat.

30

Her silence didn't dampen his spirits. A good woman didn't need to be a chatterbox. As she took in the river and the beauty of the hillsides, he had difficulty taking his eyes from her. She was poised, beautiful, and sure of herself. All traits that he admired. He was startled when she made a sudden turn to see the ivory handle of a knife that was tucked into a sheath in the fold of her dress and behind the shawl. He stifled a smile; not only was she sure of herself but she was prepared to defend herself. His admiration for this vivacious young woman grew.

A few minutes later she pointed to what appeared to be some rocky ruins scattered along the hillside above the river. "What are those?" she said as she looked up at him.

"I'm not sure," he said. "They appear to be very old."

A man, who was standing nearby spoke, as he looked at the couple. "Those are the ruins of the Seneca Indian village. That's where Queen Aliquippa once held sway for many years. She died nearly fifty years ago. She was a fine old Indian woman who led her people for many years."

"How interesting," exclaimed Hannah. "Thank you for telling us about the ruins and the Indian woman, Aliquippa."

They remained standing at the bow of the boat as it moved downstream. The river twisted and turned, and its meanderings brought new vistas with each turn. Jean left off viewing the scenery and turned to the vivacious young girl that stood at his side. "Where are you from Hannah and where are you and your parents headed?"

Her eyes left the river, and she looked up at him with a broad smile that seemed to express her happiness and determination. "We're from a small town in up-state New York," she said. Pa had a general merchandise store there, but he got restless, and when the war ended, and the peace treaty was signed with the British, he decided to sell out and move west to a new settlement called Olive Hill in Kentucky. Pa has purchased a lot there and is going to open up a store when we get there. He believes he'll do very well catering

31

to the settlers and travelers that are coming west." She smiled up at Jean as she said, "And where are you from and where are you going?"

I'm from Vermont and I'm on my way to the Blue Valley in the Ohio Territory to stake my claim to some land that has been awarded to me due to my service during the war."

"Oh, that's nice." She paused for a moment, as she looked up at him with questioning eyes, "You appear to be traveling alone. Are you married?"

"Yes, I'm all alone and no, I'm not married" He was tempted to ask her to be his wife, so as to remedy the latter deficiency, but he restrained himself. After all, he had met her only a few hours ago.

They stood side by side at the railing. She was so close that he could smell her perfume, which seemed to have an intoxicating effect on him, as would a glass of hard, home brewed liquor. There was no headache, but otherwise the effect was much the same.

They continued to stand at the railing as the boat docked at the small settlement of Buffalo Creek to take on a supply of lumber to be delivered downstream to the new settlement of Marietta, located on the Ohio side of the river. They tarried at Buffalo Creek for only a couple of hours and then continued the journey along the winding twisting river, skirting sand bars and small islands. Ducks, geese and a variety of waterfowl were present along the river, fluttering up into the air with flapping wings and loud squawks as the flatboat came near. They frequently saw deer, elk, and an occasional bear feeding along the shoreline. She continued to stand close as she plied him with questions, always accompanied with shy smiles and an occasional giggle. His intoxication with this lovely young woman only increased as the morning passed.

Shortly after noon they returned to the cabin and ordered sandwiches. Hannah was effusive as she described the scenery and landscape of the river to her parents. "It's a lovely and beautiful country, Pa, and I'm excited to get to our destination."

Her father smiled back at her as he said, "Yes, I'm anxious to arrive at our new home." He looked up at LaBerge and there was a wide grin across his face as he said, "Perhaps we could persuade this fine young man to accompany us to our destination."

Hannah's eyes seemed to have taken on a glow as she looked at Jean. "Oh, that would be nice! Could you change your plans, Mr. LaBerge?"

The temptation to accept the offer was strong, almost overpowering, but the return to the cabin and the presence of her parents had dissipated some of the intoxication that had overcome him at the boat railing when she had stood so close. He shook his head as he said, "I'm afraid not as I have three shares of land, twelve hundred acres, to claim. I must continue on to the Blue Valley."
He thought he detected a crestfallen look come across her face, but she said nothing as her father replied, "Yes, I understand, but it has been most pleasant making your acquaintance and we look forward to seeing you over the course of the next few days before we must part."

This acknowledgment that there would be a parting seemed to bring an end to the easy conversation and an uneasy silence fell around the table as they ate their sandwiches.

When they had finished eating their lunch, Jean and Hannah once again found a place along the bow of the flatboat and continued to watch the progress of their journey.

Inside the cabin Jedidiah turned to his wife as he said, "I like that young man and am sorry we will part within a few days, but of course he must continue on to his destination and claim his land." He smiled at his wife. "I can see that he is a decisive man and I predict that he will be a man of some substance someday."

"Yes, he is a real gentleman." She smiled at her husband as she continued, "And he would make a fine husband for our daughter."
"Yes, I agree, but it appears that we will soon part and will probably never see him again. It's a shame."

The afternoon slipped by as the flatboat glided along the winding Ohio River, past ever-changing hills and mountains. In a rather bold move, LaBerge took her hand and lead her to the rear of the boat and introduced her to his horse, burro, and Shag. The dog had fallen asleep on a small pile of straw but was overjoyed to see his master, and he immediately jumped to his feet and greeted them with a vigorous wagging of his tail. Hannah bent and patted him on the head which only intensified the movement of his tail.

Jean and Hannah stood at the rail and watched the sun slip behind the darkening hills as a soft evening breeze tugged at the edges of her bonnet. The breeze picked up a chill from the water and Jean removed his jacket and draped it about her shoulders. "We probably should go in before long," he said.

He could barely see her smile as she looked up at him. "Not yet, I want to see the stars come out. Let's wait a little while before we go in."

They moved close to the railing and looked up at the vast velvet of the evening sky and watched with delight as the sky filled with stars until it bespoke a tapestry that no man could weave. There were few passengers about, and the darkness was deep, broken only by a few lanterns that hung about the cabin of the boat. Her perfume rose up to him again and he had to fight the strong temptation to gather her into his arms and kiss her. He shook off the urge. He had promised her father that he would protect her, not make advances toward her.

She looked up at him and in the dim light from a lantern he could see the smile on her face and the sparkle in her eyes as she said. "It's so lovely," she whispered.

The night breeze had now become cold. "We better go in," he said.

"Yes, I suppose so, but I like watching the night sky and the stars with you. You have been very kind to me and my family."

Hannah's father had rented one of the small rooms in the cabin for his family and soon after Jean and Hannah returned to the cabin they retired to their room. LaBerge paid the man behind the counter fifty cents for a cot and a slice of meat for his dog and then walked to the back of the boat where he set the cot up near his animals. He retrieved the bear coat, pulled off his shirt and lay down on the cot with the coat pulled up against the chill of the evening. Shag wolfed down the meat and then curled up under the cot.

The movement of the flatboat along the river quickly lulled him to sleep, but his dreams were filled with the image of a lovely young lady whose perfume overpowered him.

Three days later when the riverboat docked at the frontier settlement of Huntington, Jean LaBerge had become much better acquainted with Hannah Cody and his desire to ask her to marry him had not diminished, and had only grown. He assisted Mr. Cody in unloading his oxen and wagon from the riverboat and then accompanied them to the west edge of the settlement, where a small group of travelers were assembling to travel on west together.

A huge bonfire was built and after a large quantity of food had been consumed a man produced a fiddle and another a harmonica, and dancing and laughter began. Within moments Jean had swept Hannah up into his arms and was twirling her about the campfire. To hold her in his arms left this tall man from Vermont breathless but saddened, as they would part tomorrow. Perhaps he would never see her again. The very thought of it left him filled with melancholy.

When the first dance ended, he led her to the edge of the camp and behind a wagon. She didn't resist his efforts to lead her away from the fire and the crowd. In the darkness at the edge of the wagon he looked down at her as he said. "Hannah, we go our separate ways tomorrow. We may never meet again."

She stood very close to him and the dim light from the moon played across the smile on her face as she looked up at him. "Yes, I . . . I wish we didn't have to part."

Here in the soft moonlight, with the music of the fiddle and harmonica wafting across the evening, her tender beauty was too much for him to resist and in an instant, he pulled her close and kissed her lips. She didn't resist as her arms entwined his shoulders and she returned the kiss. When they drew apart, she sighed and laid her head on his shoulder.

After a moment he held her away as he said, "Hannah, when I'm settled in the Blue Valley, may I come to Kentucky, to Olive Hill, to see you?"

Her eyes were sparkling in the moonlight as she exclaimed, "Yes Jean, I would like that. Please come and see me as soon as you can."

CHAPTER 5

Hunted

Jean LaBerge stepped over to the little branch that flowed down from a crack in the limestone and had a drink; then he went to a place he could sit with his back against a rock wall with his long rifle across his knees. He'd eaten a sparse, late evening meal of dried jerky and bread and washed it down with the cold water from the spring. The wind came down through the oak and sycamore trees, moaning a lonesome song which matched his mood, as he leaned back against the rock wall.

He settled in and got himself comfortable. From where he sat, he commanded a wide view of the tree and shrub covered hillside below his camp. Oak, sycamore, and elm trees grew along the hillside and willows and poplar along the banks of the stream as it flowed away down the incline and toward the river. The sun had slipped below the sharp hills to the west, nearly an hour past, and his campsite was now shrouded in the deep gray of the on-coming night. When he looked up at the night sky his gaze was rewarded with the sight of a myriad of stars that seemed to be dancing across the endless velvet of the night sky. A pale, quarter-moon hung low in the western sky. He shifted his gaze from the stars and to the remnants of the campfire. Only a few faint coals could be seen in the darkness. His dog, Shag, lay at the edge of the dying campfire, his head resting on his paws.

He was tired and craved sleep and was tempted to spread out his bedroll and let the dog guard the camp. The dog would warn him of anyone approaching during the night. The bedroll was enticing, and he had confidence in his dog, but his instincts told him that the men would come during the night, and he planned to be awake and prepared, when they came.

The night wore on and the pale crescent moon followed the sun, as it slid silently behind the hills, deepening the dark gloom shrouding his campsite. There were times when he almost dozed off and to keep awake, he tried to bring memories back, something to keep his mind busy. His thoughts quickly drifted to the willow girl he had met on the flatboat. Her dancing eyes were dark brown, and her dark hair hung in long curls about her shoulders below the bonnet she wore. Her smiling laugh was infectious and her skin a smooth, olive tone. He wondered where she was now and what she was doing? Had she and her family made it safely through to their destination of Olive Hill, Kentucky, or had the five men abducted them. When he thought of the five men he was filled with apprehension and concern for Hannah and her family.

The five men had ridden into the settler's camp, near Huntington, shortly after the dance had ended and the bonfire was dying down. The settlers had watched in silence as the five men had ridden in on worn and ill-fed nags and staked out a campsite for themselves. They had talked rough and bragged on their past exploits during the war of independence. LaBerge knew that men who had seen real action, during the bloody years of the war, seldom bragged of what they had done. He knew their type; weak and lazy men, who he strongly suspected preyed on others.

LaBerge had observed one of the men, a man his companions had referred to as Kilkenny, lay roaming and covetous eyes on Hannah, although he had made no direct effort to even speak with her. LaBerge had quickly discerned his motives and he had kept a careful watch on Kilkenny and his companions during the late evening and night, and until the men had left the camp the next morning. They had ridden west, in the direction that the settlers were headed with their wagons, horses, and belongings. They had not tried to molest, harm, or steal from any of the travelers while they were in camp.

LaBerge was of the opinion that the large number of settlers, and perhaps his own presence, had discouraged the men from any such skullduggery. However, LaBerge had seen such men before and he was of the opinion that they intended to lay in wait for those they thought they could overpower, including Hannah and her family, and rob them of their money and valuables.

He had spoken to Jedidiah Cody of his concerns about these men, suggesting they delay their departure to put some distance between them and the five men. Her father had assured LaBerge that he would remain alert, that they would be traveling with a number of other settlers, which would afford them safety in numbers. LaBerge had taken a liking to her parent's but felt that Hannah's father was a little naive about people, especially the likes of these men.

LaBerge had assisted Mr. Cody in removing the oxen and wagon from the riverboat and Cody had confided to LaBerge that the carpet bag contained all of his money and that he had a secret compartment in the floor of the wagon where the bag was hidden while traveling. LaBerge's concerns for the wellbeing of Hannah and her parents were heightened by his knowledge of this money. If the ruffians were unable to locate Cody's money it was possible that they would kidnap the family until Cody told them where the money was hidden.

The hushed darkness of the night seemed to deepen his anxiety for the willowy girl, and he was of the opinion that he should have altered his own plans and remained with them until they reached their destination, and he was disgusted with himself for this lapse in following his instincts.

He suddenly left off musing of the girl, shifted his position and stared intently into the darkness, alert, his rifle at the ready as it lay across his knees. His instincts, and years living by his wits, had alerted him that he was no longer alone; a twig had snapped, and the chirping of the crickets had been broken. The men who had been following him were out there in the darkness, plotting and waiting. Twice today he'd caught a fleeting glimpse of at least two men, perhaps more, he couldn't be sure, on his back trail. He couldn't be sure, but he suspected that the men trailing him were a part of the five men that had rode into the settler's camp. Why had they broken away and were now trailing him? Perhaps they had discerned that he wore a money belt and had seen that his burro was heavily laden.

Suddenly the dog lifted his head from his paws. He looked about and then a low growl came from deep in his chest.

"Easy, boy!" LaBerge whispered. "Easy now!"

LaBerge continued to sit, listening, trying to separate the casual sounds of the night from the sound that had alerted the dog. Several minutes slipped by as both he and the dog remained silent and alert, listening into the night.

Suddenly he discerned a shadow of movement, near an oak tree, just below where he sat, perhaps fifty yards away. The movement had been only a fleeting shadow, barely discernable in the deep darkness of the night. He held his long rifle at the ready but didn't cock it. The sound could be heard sharp, in the silence of the night, and he didn't want to alert the men, who lurked in the shadows.

The low wind continued to stir the leaves and moan through the trees as he rose carefully to his feet. His mouth was dry, and he could feel his heart beating, slow and heavy. Someone was moving below him, near the big oak tree.

The dog came suddenly to his feet, staring into the darkness of the night, his eyes intent on a spot about forty yards away at the edge of a stand of willows growing along the bank of the stream, as he growled, low and deep. So, mused LaBerge, there were two men out there.

And then a voice cut through the silence of the night, "Hello, the camp!" The voice came from the darkness below him, and he thought from the man who stood near the oak. The man spoke again, "I know it's late, but may I come on in? A cup of coffee would sure go down well for a tired man."

LaBerge recognized the voice of the man. He was one of the five men, a short, stout man with broad shoulders, a fat round face and a heavy beard, who had ridden into the settler's camp at Huntington.

LaBerge made no reply to this salutation and his voice was barely above a whisper as he spoke to the dog. "Take it easy boy, I'll tell you when to go."

He stared down into the darkness toward the oak. The man had said, *"May I come on in?"* implying there was only one man, but LaBerge trusted his dog; there were two of them. One near the oak and the other in the willows. They had come for him. Two against one probably seemed to be pretty good odds to the men.

LaBerge eased to his left and moved into deeper darkness as he surveyed the oak and the stand of willows that sheltered the two men. He surmised that the five men had the girl and her family. He was sure of it, and at least two of the men had broken away and come for his money belt, his animals, and the pack that lay next to the remnants of the fire. They were all a no-good lot. He felt his anger boiling up into his throat and his grip increased on the long rifle as a calm determination flooded through him.

The campfire was nearly dead now, with only a few faintly glowing coals remaining and the night was gripped by a deep, silent darkness. Once again, he whispered to the dog. "Hold still Shag. I'll tell you when to go." The dog eased down again onto his belly, but his eyes never left the clump of willows. He continued to emit low, intermittent growls.

LaBerge moved on silent moccasin feet along the rock wall, and then down and away from his campsite. Crouching low he moved from boulder to boulder and then to bushes and trees until he was within twenty feet of the big oak and then he spoke, "Lean your long rifle against the tree and step out where I can see you."

There was a long silence and then the man said, "You're an unfriendly cuss. I mean no harm and am only looking for a place to bed down for the night and maybe a cup of coffee, if you can spare one."

"If what you say is true then you shouldn't be afraid of leaning your gun against the tree and stepping out into the open." He paused for a moment and then continued, "And the same goes for your partner who is over there in the willows." He raised his voice. "You there, in the willows. Step out from the willows so I can see you."

The man behind the oak didn't move as he said, "I've got no partner. I'm traveling alone. You're just a bit jumpy this evening. And besides, I don't know you, so why would I want to do a fool thing like step out and leave my rifle behind?"

And then LaBerge heard the sharp click as the man under the oak cocked his gun. In a swift movement he dived hard to his left and yelled, "Get him Shag!" The shot from the long rifle shattered the silence of the night but missed LaBerge by a good margin. He was on his feet in an instant as he rushed the man before he could unsheathe his knife. The knife hadn't cleared the scabbard when he hit him, low down and hard, knocking him sprawling, the knife falling into the leaves and dirt. LaBerge was strong and agile and within a few moments he had the man in a hammer lock, grinding his face into the dirt with his knee jammed into his back. He held the man down with his knee as he quickly bound his wrists and ankles with a strip of rawhide. While he was about this task, he could hear the growls of his dog and the screams and oaths of the second man from the willows.

He shoved the man up against a tree as he said, "That will hold you for now, while I attend to your partner in the willows. It sounds like he could use a little help getting shut of my dog."

He stood to his feet and strode to the clump of willows. He had to suppress a laugh. The man was flat on his back as he flailed his arms and legs in a desperate attempt to ward off the snarling dog. LaBerge picked up the man's rifle from where it had fallen and then said, "Okay Shag, that's enough; let him up."

With obvious reluctance the dog backed away. The man slowly pulled himself into a sitting position as he looked up at LaBerge. His hands were torn and bleeding. His face was cut, and a heavy stream of blood ran down his nose and chin. His buckskin shirt was nearly shredded. "Get up," said LaBerge.

When the man was on his feet LaBerge stepped forward and jerked his knife from the sheath at the man's waist. He prodded him toward the big oak and his partner.

When they were at the oak, LaBerge shoved the man down beside his partner and then tied his hands behind his back. He stood looking down at the two men for a long moment and then he said, "I see that you've separated from your friends in crime to come looking for me." A faint smile came to his face as he continued. "It turns out that didn't work out so well for the two of you." He paused for a moment, glanced at his dog and then back down at the two men. "I think your partners have taken the Cody family prisoners. Is that correct?"

The two men said nothing as they stared up at him through the gloom of the night. LaBerge jerked the two men to their feet, took up his rifle and the men's weapons and then pushed them up the incline to his camp. He pushed them down on a log and said to his dog. "Watch them Shag. Eat 'em alive if they move!"

He took up wood and threw it on the remnants of the fire and watched as it caught and blazed high, lighting his campsite. He made his way back down toward the oak and the willows and soon found the men's horses tied a short distance away. He led them back to camp and pulled their saddles.

The two men watched in silence as he undertook these chores. When he was finished, he squatted down in front of the two men and looked into their questioning eyes as he said, "You men tell me where your partners have taken the girl and her family or I'll take your weapons, your horses, and your boots, and leave you here to make it out on your own. We're a long way from a settlement and are in Shawnee and Iroquois Indian country. Give me your answer in the morning." He cast a glance at his dog who stood nearby, his teeth bared as low growls continued from his throat. "Keep a watch on them Shag. I'm gonna catch a couple of hours of sleep and then I'll watch."

CHAPTER 6

Prisoners

Hannah Cody griped the side of the wagon in an effort to keep her balance. Her hands and shoulders were bruised and sore from the constant jostling of the wagon. Her teeth were clinched in anger and frustration at what had happened to her and her family. The wagon bounced over an especially rough rut in the trail, and she had to grab the side of the wagon with both hands to keep from being knocked to the floor. Anger and determination welled up anew in her heart. She was determined to do something to escape from these evil men who had taken them captive.

She was seated on the floor of the wagon, her back to the tailgate, as the wagon bumped along the trail. Her father lay near the center of the wagon, his hands and feet bound with rawhide. Her mother had placed a pillow under his head to give him a measure of comfort during the rough ride up the mountainside. From time to time her father glanced along the wagon at her, his eyes filled with remorse and fear. She could almost read his thoughts: *I'm sorry Hannah, I should have listened to that tall stranger, Jean LaBerge.* Her mother sat on a small crate next to her father. Her hands and feet were free, but Hannah could see the fear in her eyes as she clutched the edge of the wagon in an effort to avoid being thrown to the floor of the wagon.

One of their captors, who the other two men addressed as Kilkenny, sat on the high seat at the front of the wagon. As Hannah looked forward, he uttered an oath and snapped the whip at the brace of oxen pulling the wagon, "Get a move on you fool animals. Can't ya move any faster?" The slow steady pace of the two oxen remained

44

unchanged; a snapping whip meant little to them. The oxen and wagon moved along a narrow road, which was little more than a wide trail that had been hacked out of the steep mountain wilderness. When they had been captured, they had been told they were being taken to a place Kilkenny had referred to as the *Roost*. The name meant nothing to her or her family.

Looking past Kilkenny and the oxen, she could see the second man, Taggert, riding his scrawny gray mare as he led them up the mountain. Taggert was a short, rather non-descript man, clad in dirty clothing, with a perpetual scowl on his lean, bewhiskered face. Taggert had said very little during their journey up the mountain, but he was one of their captors and she loathed him.

She watched Kilkenny and Taggert for several minutes, as the journey carried them further into the mountains. As she watched Kilkenny's back and listened to his oaths directed at the oxen, her anger rose, and she was once again filled with a renewed determination to escape and attempt to find help. Unconsciously her hand went to the knife in the fold of her dress. The men hadn't searched her, or her mother, and the knife gave her a measure of comfort, especially for her personal safety from the unwanted advances of any of these men.

After a few minutes she scooted around and looked back over the tailgate at the third man who made up their three captors. She had heard his companions refer to him as Keaton. He rode a pale dune horse, that if properly fed and groomed, would pass as a fair horse. Keaton appeared somewhat younger than his two companions. He had shaved within the past few days, and it appeared that he made a passing effort to maintain a decent appearance. A tattered hat sat askew on his head and his buckskin shirt and pants were worn and patched. A knife was buckled about his waist, and he held a long rifle that lay across the saddle in front of him.

She continued to watch Keaton with a mild interest as they bounced and jostled along the rough road. It seemed to Hannah's discerning eyes that he rode with disinterested and sad eyes that were shadowed and cast down at the trail in front of his horse. He had said little during their capture, remaining silent and uncommunicative as he took directions from Kilkenny. Hannah wondered about him. He didn't seem to fit in with the other two men.

She continued to watch Keaton with mild curiosity for several minutes, and then she turned again to look at her father. Her father had made a serious mistake when he had separated from the two families they had been traveling with. As they had traveled west from Huntington, several wagons, and their occupants, had dropped out as they reached the turnoffs to their destinations, until there were only three wagons and families remaining. They had traveled together for another day and had then parted. Hannah and her parents had proceeded on in their lone wagon for a day and were camped along a slow flowing stream near the edge of a green meadow when the five men had come into their camp an hour before sunrise, while they were still sleeping.

There had been no fight, the men had them surrounded, their long rifles cocked and at the ready. Hannah and her parents had little choice but to surrender to the men. Kilkenny had done most of the talking as he had confronted her father, demanding their money and valuables. Under the scowls and threats of the men, her mother had handed over her cherished broach, which she had inherited from her mother, and her father had given Kilkenny his pocket watch had belonged to his father. She had reluctantly given Kilkenny the broach her mother had given her on her eighteenth birthday. In addition, her father had taken out his wallet and handed Kilkenny all of his cash money of about fifty dollars.

Kilkenny had surveyed these items for a moment, had stuffed the money into a pocket, and then stepped forward to face her father, as he demanded, "Where's the rest of yer money? I know ya have got a wad of money with ya. I heard ya telling some folks that ya had sold yer store and were headin' west. So, ya have got to have some money with ya, besides this little bit of cash ya gave me. He took another step forward and his face was only a few inches from her father's as he had yelled, "Give me the money or I'll bash yer head in!" Before they had left New York, her father had constructed a hiding place in the floor of the wagon. He had placed the several thousand dollars he had received from the sale of the store into a carpet bag and the bag was now hidden in the floor of the wagon. Her father had not flinched as he had replied, "I am not carrying any additional cash. The proceeds from the sale of the store are on deposit in a bank in New York."

Kilkenny had stared at her father for several moments and had then turned to Taggert and Keaton as he exclaimed, "Go through the wagon and make sure he's not lying."

The two men had ransacked the wagon but hadn't found the hiding place of the satchel. Taggert had called down from the rear of the wagon, "There's no money here! We've about torn her apart. I think he's tellin' ya the truth."

Kilkenny had stomped about the camp, his face filled with anger. Several minutes passed and then he whirled as he said, "Yer comin' with us. We'll take ya to the Roost and ya can write for the money to be sent to ya." Her father's protests had been ignored.

Within half an hour they had broken camp. Kilkenny drove the wagon, her father lay on the floor, his hands and feet tied.

As they were preparing to leave the camp Kilkenny had taken two of his men aside and she had heard them conversing in low tones. She had been unable to hear their conversation, but she felt sure she had heard Kilkenny mention the name of the tall stranger, Jean LaBerge. Within a few minutes the two men had mounted their horses and rode away, in a northerly direction. The two men had not returned.

She suspected the two men had been sent to capture or kill Jean LaBerge. A shudder coursed through her heart as she remembered how he had assisted them at the flatboat. Her lips seemed to burn with the memory of the stolen kiss in the shadows at the edge of the campfire. And then she had smiled to herself; two men against one were not good odds, but she had seen enough of the tall man from Vermont to know that he could likely outwit those two men. She suspected that those two men were in for a surprise when they found LaBerge.

47

Hannah continued to stare out the rear of the wagon, watching Keaton as he rode behind them, his eyes cast down to the ground. After a while she let her eyes roam up to the tree covered hills and mountains and she watched a hawk as it circled across the deep blue sky. She was a captive of these three men and the hawk was free. As she watched the big bird glide through the blue sky a vague and growing hope began to spring up in her heart. If LaBerge outwitted the two men, or captured them, he would most likely discern that she and her family had been taken captive. She had only known him for a few days, but it had been time enough to discern that he was a man of action and integrity. If he learned of their plight, she was sure he would come to rescue her and her parents.

Their progress slowed as the oxen labored up a particularly steep incline, and once again she could hear Kilkenny yell oaths at the oxen. With each jerk and sway of the wagon her anger and determination welled up higher in her heart. She must escape from these evil men and find help for her and her parents. She could not be sure that the tall stranger would come to rescue her and her family. Escaping from these vile men wouldn't be easy, but she was determined to try. It would be dark in a few hours, and they would be making camp soon. If some luck came her way, perhaps she could slip out of the camp tonight. She had seen a lone cabin shortly before they had turned from the trail that followed a creek and had begun the ascent up this rough road. Perhaps she could make her way to this cabin and would find someone there who would be willing to help her rescue her parents.

She was determined to find help for her Ma and Pa, but she was driven to escape for a second reason. She was young, pretty, and shapely and she had no illusions as to the designs of these men upon her. She had seen and noted the lust in the eyes of Kilkenny. If she were unable to escape, or if advances were made upon her, she had the long knife, its blade always honed as sharp as a razor, tucked in a small scabbard inside her dress where she could quickly reach through the folds to fetch it. She would use the knife with all of her strength to protect herself. The hoped that the man who attacked her would look like a gutted fish when she was finished with him.

At eighteen years of age Hannah Cody was a bit small for her age. Most of her friends said she was as cute as a button, smart as a whip, and with a right pert figure. But no mind her slight stature, she made up for this deficiency, with an extra helping of spunk and determination.

By nature, an adventurous young girl, she had been delighted when her parents had decided to sell their general merchandise store and move to the new pioneer settlement of Olive Hill, Kentucky. The war of independence had finally come to an end, the peace treaty signed with the British, and now, many of the restless residents of the former colonies were leaving for the frontier, and many were going to Ohio and Kentucky.

The oxen plodded on and the swaying of the wagon slowly lulled Hannah into a fitful slumber. As she dozed a blurry vision of a tall, handsome man, dressed in fresh buckskin, flashed briefly through her mind. She called out to him as he rode away from her: "*Come back. Come back and help us!*" She awoke with a start as the wagon jolted to a sudden halt and the vision of the tall man suddenly vanished as she heard Kilkenny yell, "We'll make camp here for the night."

Hannah shook the sleep from her eyes as she pushed herself up to a sitting position and looked forward. She watched as Kilkenny jumped from the seat to the ground and disappear from sight. She stood to her feet and watched as he unhooked the oxen from the wagon tongue, removed their yokes and then pushed them away toward a patch of grass next to a small stream. The oxen immediately went to the water and drank and then began to graze. Within a few minutes Kilkenny appeared at the rear of the wagon. A whiskered grin covered his face as he said, "You folks get out and help with fixin' something to eat." He looked past Hannah at her father. "I'll untie yer hands and feet if you give me yer word that you'll not try to escape or undertake some other foolish action. If you do, you'll regret it."

Her father stared at Kilkenny with tired and worn eyes for a long moment and then he said, "Yes, I'll give you, my word. Laying here in the wagon most all day, with my hands and feet bound, has about done me in and I don't know what foolishness I could engage in. I'm no gunman; only a storekeeper."

Kilkenny fumbled with the latches and then lowered the rear gate to the wagon. He started to extend a hand to Hannah, but she had turned and gone to her mother. "Here Ma, take my hand, I'll help you out of the wagon."

When they arrived at the back of the wagon she jumped to the ground and then helped her mother down. "Wait here," she said. "I'll untie Pa's hands and feet."

Kilkenny remained standing at the end of the wagon. "I'll untie him," he said.

Hannah drew herself up to her full height of five feet, four inches as she looked at him with piercing eyes. "No, I'll tend to my Pa. You go on about whatever you need to do. We'll be along in a few minutes to help with fixing something to eat." She paused as she continued to hold him in a steady gaze. He might as well understand that even though they were his prisoners, they were not cowed and had not relinquished their dignity.

He looked at her for a long moment, as if he were considering how to respond to her, and then abruptly turned and strode away as he shook his head.

She turned to her mother, "Wait here Ma, until I get Pa untied. I think it best for the three of us to stick together."

As she untied her father's hands she whispered in a low voice. "What are we going to do Pa? "If they find our money, they may kill us."

Her father sat up and rubbed his wrists as she untied his ankles, "Yes, they're a hard lot, and you are probably right. I've been thinking some on it. We're in a bad situation and we need time. Time for help to come. My first goal is to keep us alive. I think I have an idea that may buy us some time."

She helped her father from the wagon. He stood for a long moment behind the wagon, stomping his feet and rubbing his wrists to regain circulation. "My feet are as numb as tree stumps," he exclaimed.

The three of them stood for several moments as they took in the campsite their captors had chosen. Hannah had to admit that it was an attractive place. It was near a little gurgling stream with shade trees nearby. The oxen and horses grazed on the lush grass that bordered the stream. Her father took her and her mother's arms as he said, "Let's stay together and see what we can do to help. There is nothing to be gained by antagonizing these men unnecessarily."

Taggert and Keaton came into the camp, each bearing an armload of firewood and within a few minutes Keaton had a fire blazing. Hannah and her mother worked to prepare biscuits and a pot of stew. An hour later they all sat on several downed logs as they ate their evening meal in the gathering twilight. As they were cleaning up the last of the meal, Hannah's father spoke to the three men as he directed his comments at Kilkenny. "I know you said you were taking us to a place you referred to as the Roost. Where is this place?"

Kilkenny sat passively on the log as he looked at Cody. "The Roost is a sort of a hideout for a man named Belle Turk and his men. It's located in a secluded and hard to get to spot high up on this mountain. The trail's rough and those oxen are slower than molasses in January. We'll be there sometime tomorrow, or the day after."

Cody stood to his feet and stepped forward to within a few feet of Kilkenny. He looked down on the bandit as he said, "I'll agree to write to the bank in New York and request the money. I'm sure it will take several weeks for the letter to be posted and a draft for the funds returned to me. Do you give me your word that you will release us when you have the money?"

Kilkenny snickered as he stood to his feet, a sly grin across his face as he faced Cody. "You write the letter as soon as we get to the Roost, and I'll see that it gets posted and on its way. I'm gonna keep you captive until the money you have in New York has been sent to you and you have turned it over to us. I'll let you go then."

He paused for a moment and his eyes rested for a fleeting instant on Hannah and then he continued, "You'll get me the money, or you and your family will pay dearly, in ways I don't think you would like, Mr. Cody."

Cody looked at Kilkenny. "I'll write the letter as soon as we get to this place you call the Roost."

Hannah's father stepped back to the log, sat down and took up his plate. He took a bite from his biscuit and a large helping of the stew. He wanted to smile to himself, but he refrained from such an obvious gesture. He hoped he had bought some time for him and his family. Sending a letter to his old bank in New York, where he no longer had an account, wouldn't get Kilkenny any money. He had bought them some time, but they must find a way of escaping from these men. His mind drifted to the tall man who helped board his oxen and cart onto the flatboat and who had introduced himself as Jean LaBerge. It was a long shot, but perhaps this near stranger would come to their rescue.

CHAPTER 7

Assaulted

H annah Cody stumbled along near the rear of the wagon. Each step was an uphill struggle to gain footing on the rough trail. Her shoes were scuffed and torn, and her feet and legs throbbed with pain.

She glanced forward to where her parents walked beside the wagon, each with an arm grasping the side of the wagon in an effort to keep from falling. The trail was a steep, rock strewn track of deep ruts and holes, which made walking difficult and almost impossible for the passage of a team of oxen and a wagon. Hannah could see that her mother was gasping for breath and when she would glance back at Hannah, she could see beads of perspiration on her mother's forehead. Her father walked behind her mother and at times reached forward and put his hand on her shoulder to steady her. She was sure that her parents must be very tired and worn from the hard, uphill walk that had gone on for hours, with hardly a pause. Hannah glanced up at the sun with a vague hope that it was about to slide behind the mountain, signaling the end of the treacherous day and they would make camp.

The sound of the cracking whip came to her from the front of the wagon, and she could hear Kilkenny as he cursed at the oxen. That morning, as they had prepared to resume their journey up the mountain, Kilkenny had said, "The trail becomes steeper and poorer as we go on up the mountain. It'll be tough going and we may not reach the Roost today."

She loathed Kilkenny, but in this he had told the truth. The trail was virtually impassable for the wagon. Even at the slow pace set by the oxen, she was surprised the wagon held together as it was jostled over the rocks and potholes. As they slowly rounded a sharp turn in the trail, she caught a glimpse of Taggert as he led the way up the mountain. Taggert glanced back at the wagon with dull eyes and a tired and worn expression on his face. For a moment, their eyes met and then he looked away.

Taggert appeared to be about twenty-five years of age, although it was difficult to be sure, as these men lived rough lives and were probably younger than they looked. There were a couple of holes near the top of Taggert's hat and heavy sweat stains covered the lower half of the hat. His buckskin shirt and pants were frayed and worn and were obviously several years old. She wondered if they were the only clothing he owned.

Taggert had said little since their capture, although she had detected a distinct British accent on the few occasions when he had spoken. His eyes were nearly expressionless and impossible to read. Hannah had an inquisitive mind and she wondered where Taggert was from and why he had allied himself with such a man as Kilkenny. Perhaps Taggert was a deserter from the British army, who had fallen in with Kilkenny when circumstances had turned against him. She knew that many men had deserted from the Red Coats. Most of the British soldiers were forced draftees from the poor and disadvantaged class of England and were treated with distain and harshness by their officers. She had been told that many of the deserters carried whip marks across their backs. The thought made her shudder. She began to wonder just how loyal Taggert, and Keaton were to Kilkenny. Would they actually put their lives on the line for him?

Within moments Taggert was lost from her view and she turned her attention back to her parents. The rough trail was especially difficult for her mother. She didn't know how much further Kilkenny would take them today, but she hoped they would make camp before her mother gave out. She winced suddenly as she felt a sharp pebble in her shoe. She quickly stopped walking, sat down on a rock, pulled off her shoe, and removed the small stone. As she tugged

54

her shoe back on, Keaton, who had been bringing up the rear of the little caravan, stopped his horse and looked down at her. "You doin' alright ma'am?"

When she looked up at him, she thought she detected a faint smile on his face. "Yes, I needed to remove a pebble that got into my shoe."

"Yeah, ya can't walk with a rock in yer shoe."

When she stood to her feet, she looked up at him as she said, "My Ma is about done in. We need to stop for the night."

Keaton said nothing for a long moment as he looked down at her and then he said, "Kilkenny's the boss. I guess we'll stop when he wants to. Not much I can do, ma'am."

She started to walk away and then she turned back to Keaton and her voice was filled with a hardness as she said, "You men are little better than animals to treat us this way." She stepped to the front of his horse and drew herself up to her full height. Her eyes were filled with determination and fire as she said, "You may think we are helpless and can't fight back, but mark my word, there will come a day of reckoning for you and your kind. You will pay and pay dearly!"

He stared down at her for a long moment, surprised at her outburst and threat, and then his eyes left hers as he looked straight ahead at the receding wagon. He said nothing as he spurred his horse and rode on.

Hannah watched his back as he rode away, a little surprised at what she had just said, and she was unsure how to interpret his failure to respond, and in suddenly riding away. She stared at him for a long moment and then hurried forward to catch the wagon.

She was breathing hard when she caught up with the wagon, and she grabbed the tail gate as she gasped for breath. The pebble was gone from her shoe, but her feet hurt, and her heart was pounding. How much longer could they keep this up? She looked forward along the wagon and could see Keaton, who was now riding beside Kilkenny at the front of the wagon. She could see that they were conversing in low tones. Perhaps Keaton was urging Kilkenny to halt for the day. She hoped so. Perhaps she had judged him too harshly.

She continued to hang onto the tail gate as they slowly moved up the mountainside. Within a few minutes she walked past Keaton who had left his place beside Kilkenny and was waiting for the wagon to pass. He glanced at Hannah but said nothing as he pulled his horse in behind the wagon.

A half hour slipped by, and Hannah's heavy breathing had subsided when suddenly she heard a shrill cry from her mother. She quickly left the rear of the wagon and rushed forward to where her mother lay on the rocky ground at the edge of the trail. Hannah was at her side in a moment. "What is it Ma?" she exclaimed.

Her mother clutched at her ankle as she exclaimed, "I stepped on a rock and turned my ankle. Oh, it hurts like the devil!"

She looked up at Hannah. "I've got to sit here until the pains are gone. I can't walk any further!"

Her father, who had quickly knelt beside his wife, jumped to his feet and yelled at Keaton, who had stopped his horse and sat looking down at them. "Stop the wagon. My wife is injured, and she must ride inside."

Keaton said nothing but he did spur his horse forward, past the three of them, and then she heard him shout, "Hold on Kilkenny, the woman has hurt her ankle and can't walk anymore."

Hannah heard a loud oath from Kilkenny, but within moments the wagon came to a halt. A few minutes later Kilkenny stood looking down at her mother. "What's wrong?" he demanded in a harsh and questioning tone.

Cody's teeth were clinched in anger as he replied, "My wife has sprained her ankle," He was only a storekeeper but if he had possessed a weapon, he would have attempted to kill this man. He took a deep breath to check his temper as he said, "She can't walk any further and will need to ride in the wagon from here on." Cody paused for a moment and then looked at Kilkenny. "I think it best if we stop for the night as soon as possible. Surely you can show my wife a little compassion and understanding!"

Kilkenny stared at Mrs. Cody for a long moment and then said. "Suit yer self. It'll be rough as hell in the wagon." He started to turn away and then paused as he said, "We'll be at a decent place to spend the night in about a half hour." He turned abruptly and strode away toward the front of the wagon.

Hannah and her father knelt and assisted Mrs. Cody to her feet. She stood carefully on her good foot as she continued to grimace in pain. Her face was flushed, and tears ran down her face. Hannah took her hanky and cleaned her mother's face as she said, "Lean on Pa and me until the pain is a little better and then we'll get you into the wagon."

"Yes, just give me a few minutes to let the pain subside some, and to get my breath."

Hannah was surprised when she suddenly realized that Keaton stood by her side. She thought she could see some concern and softness in his eyes as he said, "Let me help get your Ma into the wagon." He glanced about and then said, "You better ride along with her to make her as comfortable as possible. It'll be a hard ride over this bad trail." He looked up at the sun. "It's late afternoon and Kilkenny said he would stop in about a half hour. Hopefully, your Ma will be better by morning."

Hannah's father stepped forward and spoke to Keaton. "I appreciate your help and concern for my wife's welfare. Thank you, young man!"

Fifteen minutes later Mrs. Cody had been helped into the wagon and they were moving again. Hannah had tucked blankets and pillows under her mother's ankle and all about her in an effort to make her as comfortable as possible and to protect her from the bouncing and swaying of the wagon. She sat near her mother for a short while and then crawled to the rear of the wagon and sat on a pillow as she gripped the sides of the wagon in an effort to steady herself against the swaying and hard jostling of the wagon as it moved along the trail. Keaton rode only a few feet behind the wagon. She smiled at him as she said in a low voice, "Thank you."

The wagon seemed to move a little slower now and Hannah thought that Kilkenny was not pushing the oxen as hard as he had before her mother had turned her ankle. The half hour past and they continued on for another twenty minutes before Kilkenny drove the oxen and wagon from the trail and into a relatively level meadow and halted beside a rushing stream. Hannah made sure her mother was as comfortable as possible and then said. "You stay here in the wagon, Ma. I'll bring you something to eat when I have some food prepared. I'll do most of the cooking. I'm afraid it won't be as good as what you would have prepared."

Mr. Cody looked in through the rear of the wagon as he said to his wife, "I'm going to get a pan of cold water from the stream and bring it here to the wagon so you can soak your ankle in it for a spell. I'm sure it will be very cold but perhaps it will help to keep the swelling down. When that's done, I'm going to tear one of my shirts into strips and bind your ankle to give it some support."

Hannah left the wagon and walked to the stream where the men were setting up camp. She stood looking at the three men for a moment and then said. "Ma can't walk with her bad ankle so I'm going to do the cooking for our evening meal." I guess I'll make up a stew and some biscuits. The meal won't be as good as what Ma would make, but I'll do the best I can."

Taggert spoke with a faint smile on his face. "We'll make do ma'am, and we're obliged to you for yer effort."

Even though she didn't admit it to herself Hannah was as good a cook as her mother and both Taggert and Keaton complimented her on the quality of the evening meal. When the meal was finished the two men even helped her clean up the pots and pans and stow everything away.

A canopy of stars covered the night sky and the campsite lay in heavy darkness except for the light from the campfire. Hannah made her way to the wagon and spent a few minutes with her parents and helped her father bind up her mother's ankle with strips of cloth from one of his shirts. She made a bed for her mother and got her comfortably situated for the night with a pillow under her ankle to keep it elevated. When these chores were completed, she took up a washrag, towel and soap and said to her parents. "I'm going to the stream and wash up a bit before I retire for the night. I'll only be gone for a few minutes."

She walked some distance from the campsite, through trees and shrubs, and then turned and went to the edge of the stream that ran swift and cold down the mountainside. She knelt at the edge of the stream and washed her arms, hands, and face. She dried her face and arms with the towel and then began to brush her hair.

She was suddenly startled by a sound that came out of the darkness. She whirled toward the sound and then she heard the low voice of Kilkenny as he stepped out from behind a tree and advanced toward her. It was dark, but in the moonlight, filtering in through the trees, she could make out the sadistic grin on his face as he said. "Well, isn't this nice, finding you all alone here. I've been watching you and you make a right curvy sight for a man to watch."

She instinctively took a step back as she exclaimed, "What do you want?"

He moved another step closer, and in the pale moonlight she could see an evil sneer on his face as he said, with a voice that seemed to project his malevolent intent. "Nothing much, just a kiss and a hug or two." He took another step closer to her as he continued, "I imagine that a few other lucky fellows have handled that body of yours. I won't be the first."

Instinctively she turned to run, but her back was to the stream. She was trapped. In her fright she dropped the hairbrush as her hand went instinctively to the knife in the fold of her skirt. Her heart was hammering as she grasped the handle of the knife. She was scared, but a cold determination came to her as she jerked the knife from its scabbard. She thrust the knife out in front of her as she exclaimed, "Stay away from me or I'll cut you with my knife! It's as sharp as Pa's razor."

Kilkenny backed away a step as he stared at the knife in her hand for only a moment. He was almost laughing as he rushed forward as he attempted to grasp her arm. "I'll get ya," he exclaimed. "Ya can't get away from me, even if ya have a knife!"

She was young and agile, and as she nimbly jumped aside, she thrust the knife hard at his ribs and was pleased when she felt the knife hit him.

He yelled in pain as he jumped back and clutched at his side. He paused for a moment as he looked down at his side. When he withdrew his hand, she could see that it was covered with blood. "You little bitch," he yelled. "I'll take more than a hug and kiss from ya now. You'll pay for this cut to my side!"

She stood with her back against the stream as she held the knife in front of her, ready to make another thrust if he came at her again. If he grabbed at her again, she hoped to cut him badly or stab the knife into his belly. "Stay away from me!" she yelled, "I'll cut you if you come at me again," She meant what she said, but she was under no illusions, he was big and strong, and unless she delivered a mortal wound, he would overpower her. She needed help.

His face was now filled with rage as he took a step toward her. "You bitch," he yelled, I'll take that knife from you and use it on you!"

She knew she must have some help and she began to scream at the top of her lungs. "Help me! Pa, Keaton, come help me!"

Kilkenny's face was filled with rage as he lunged at her, but her quick thrust of the knife made him jump back and away to the edge of the stream as he narrowly escaped another thrust from her knife. His legs were spread apart as he glared at her with hard and evil eyes. "I'll . . ."

At that moment her father, Taggert, and Keaton burst through the trees. Her father recognized instantly what was happening, and in his rage, he never hesitated as he lunged at Kilkenny. Kilkenny tried to step aside to avoid her father's charge, but he was standing in rocks at the edge of the stream, and he stumbled as he tried to jump away from Cody. Cody hit him with all of the weight of his body as he drove his shoulder into Kilkenny. Kilkenny hadn't expected such an assault from the mild-mannered storekeeper and the unexpected force of the blow knocked him sprawling into the water at the edge of the stream.

In his rage, Cody didn't hesitate as he jumped onto Kilkenny and fought to push Kilkenny's head under the rushing waters of the stream. "You bastard!" he exclaimed. "I'll drown you! You dirty swine!"

Kilkenny was a younger and stronger man than Cody and with a mighty thrust he heaved himself up from the stream, knocking Cody aside. In his rage he seemed to be oblivious to the presence of Taggart and Keaton as he yelled. "I'll kill ya Cody and then I'll rape yer daughter!"

Instinctively Hannah started to rush forward to thrust the knife into Kilkenny and protect her father and then suddenly Taggert and Keaton came to life as they jumped between Kilkenny and Cody. "Hold on Kilkenny," exclaimed Keaton. "Yer out of line coming here to assault this girl! We won't stand by and let ya carry on like this. You come with us."

"Get out of my way!" yelled Kilkenny. "I'm the boss and I won't stand for ya interfering in my doings."

"No, we won't let ya harm either Cody or the girl," exclaimed Taggart. He paused for a moment as he looked at Kilkenny. "What yer doin' is nuts. We'll never get a hold of Cody's money if ya carry on like this!"

Kilkenny stood at the edge of the stream, water dripping from his face and clothing, his fists clinched. He glared at Cody for a long moment and cast a leering glance at Hannah and then he turned and walked away through the trees and toward the camp.

Keaton turned to Hannah, a look of bewilderment on his face as he said, "I'm sorry ma'am."

Hannah's voice was barely above a whisper as she said, "Thank.
you."

Jedidiah Cody watched the three men walk away and then he bent and picked up Hannah's hairbrush, wash rag and towel. He turned to his daughter and then slipped his arm around her waist as he said, "I'll help you back to the wagon. I never should have let you come out here alone. It was stupid of me."

CHAPTER 8

Ephraim Sykes

The wind blew in a constant gale without letup. Rain spattered in his face and water dripped from the brim of his hat. He tugged the collar of his slicker up higher around his neck and ears, and then leaned forward and spread his hands before the flames of the fire.

Jean LaBerge was sheltered near the edge of a stand of trees which did little to break the insistent wind. On his left a small stream rushed past, as if eager to be on its way. The rain was falling harder now, the gusts more frequent. It would be a long and unpleasant night if the rain continued without letup.

Thirty minutes later the fire had burned down, and he stepped to a stack of wood he had covered with a small tarp in an effort to keep it dry. He pulled the tarp aside and took out several pieces of wood. He carefully laid these on the fire and watched as they slowly caught fire and the flames began to leap higher.

He reached forward and pulled the coffee pot from where it hung above the fire and poured himself a tin of coffee. The coffee was hot, and he sipped sparingly to avoid burning his tongue. When the coffee had cooled some, he wrapped his hands around the tin in an effort to keep them warm.

He cast a glance at his dog, Shag, who was sheltering near the base of an oak where he lay curled tight with his nose pushed back under his leg. He stepped to his pack and retrieved two pieces of hardtack and then took them to the dog. "Here boy," he said. "Something for you to eat." The dog's nose came up, and his mouth opened as he quickly snatched the morsels of food from his hand.

LaBerge returned to the fire and sat back down on the log. He leaned forward and once again spread his hands out toward the warmth of the fire.

The flames of the fire flashed bright against the darkness of the night. The only sound was the moan of the wind through the trees and the drip of rainwater. An hour passed and the fire slowly died to a few bright coals. He stared at the glowing coals, his mind pensive and filled with foreboding, as he thought of Hannah Cody, the malevolent men that had captured her and her parents, and the challenges that would come over the coming days.

A half hour later he shook off the melancholy and stood to his feet. He glanced up into the darkness and was pleased to note that the rain had slackened considerably. He stepped to his pack and retrieved his bedroll and walked to a flat place under the live oak and kicked the leaves back away for several feet in all directions until the wet leaves had been removed and the ground was mostly dry. He spread a small tarp out over the bare area and then laid out his bedroll on the tarp. He laid his boots, long rifle, and pistol on the tarp and then quickly removed his slicker and slid into his bedroll, pulling the blankets up over his boots and guns and nearly to his chin. If the wind didn't rise too high, he hoped to stay dry through the night.

He shuffled about to get as comfortable as possible, and then closed his eyes. Almost immediately he began to consider the challenges he faced during the coming days. The first challenge was locating the place called the Roost.

The morning, following his capture of the two men, he had fed them breakfast and then knelt in front of them and repeated his threat to leave them in the wilderness without weapons, horses, or shoes unless they told him what had happened to Hannah and her family. "It's going to be a long, hard walk out of here in your stocking feet. I'd guess your chances of making it out are less than fifty percent. If you have any sense, you'll give me this information."

The men had continued to remain mute, staring up at him with passive, dull eyes. He immediately set about breaking camp. The two men maintained their silence until they had watched him stow away their weapons and boots and then their resolve broke and one of the men began to talk.

He had glanced at his partner and then said, "Okay . . . okay! We'll tell ya what we know. We can't get out of here without our horses and boots. Yer right, Kilkenny and the other two men have got Cody, and his wife and daughter. We couldn't find any money on 'em so Kilkenny is takin' 'em to the Roost."

LaBerge had walked back to where the men were seated and looked down at them. "What do you mean by the Roost? I never heard of a settlement by that name."

"It's not a settlement or town. It's sort of a hideout for a man whose name is Belle Turk and his buddies."

"Where's this Roost located?"

The two men exchanged frightened glances and then one of them said, "It's up a tight valley in the mountains of Eastern Kentucky."

"I need better information than that!" Exasperation filled his voice. "You ever been there?"

"Yes, a few times. It's located on the north side of Flag Knob Mountain, and up above Wolf Creek. It's not an easy place ta find or ta get to."

He had stared at the two men for a long moment and then said, "How many men am I going to find when I locate this hideout?"

"I don't know," one of the men had exclaimed." Could be near a half dozen, or maybe more, just depends."

LaBerge had returned their horses, canteens, knives, and their boots to them. Each of the men had a long rifle, but he gave them only one rifle, together with powder horn and shot. One of the men had protested; "We need both rifles!"

"No, one is all you get. Only one gun will discourage you from attempting to follow me or engaging in some other foolishness. You can use the rifle to shoot a deer or turkey." He had pointed north. "You men ride north and keep going. Don't try to follow me or turn and go to the Roost. If I lay eyes on either of you again, you'll think what happened here last night was kids play against what will happen to you then."

One of the men protested, "Riding north takes us further into the wilderness and Indian country. We'd rather head south."

"That's why I want you to go north and away from most settlements. It will keep you from the settlers and the temptation to rob them. You ride two days north and then turn east. Perhaps go to the new settlement of Marietta. Hopefully, you'll have come to your senses by the time you get there."

They had grumbled at this, but he had watched as the men had ridden off to the north into the Ohio wilderness.

A light gust of wind splattered rain down onto the tall man and he pulled the slicker up over his head. That was his first challenge: how to locate the Roost.

His second challenge was a successful rescue of the Cody family when he found the Roost. One of the men had said he could expect a half dozen or more men when he found the place. Very poor odds! However, the thought of the poor odds didn't leave him filled with fear and trembling. He'd faced bad odds during the war and reached his objective.

He had been riding southeast now for two days and yesterday had sighted what he believed was Flag Knob Mountain. It was late in the day, and he had made camp on the south flank of the landmark. He was tired from the hard ride and the inclement weather. He'd work on finding the hideout called the Roost tomorrow. He closed his eyes and hunched down under the blanket and slicker and within moments he was asleep.

A gray dawn was creeping, like a sulking ghost, through his campsite when a sharp clank brought him awake. He eased himself up to a sitting position and listened. The rain had ceased during the night leaving the ground wet with pools of standing water and the trees continued to drip water. A low growl came from the dog who had jumped to his feet and was staring toward a stand of trees to his left. LaBerge eased from his bed and pulled on his boots. He reached down and took up his long rifle from inside his bed roll where he had kept it dry during the night. The gun was primed but due to the dampness of the rain he doubted if it would fire. However, the threat of the gun would be a deterrent. "Come," he whispered to the dog. Silently he slipped away from his camp and into a heavy stand of jack pine. He squatted down and the dog quickly lay down beside him.

A few minutes passed and then a man came into view as he rode out of a stand of trees. He was riding a light sorrel horse with a white blaze down his forehead and was leading a heavily laden burro. Several pots and pans, and a skillet were tied to the pack. LaBerge surmised that those utensils had been the source of the noise that had awakened him. The man came on until he spotted the camp. He halted, staring at the camp for a few moments and then called out, "Hello, the camp. Anybody about?"

LaBerge laid his hand on his dog as he whispered, "Hold on boy." LaBerge was a good judge of men and circumstances, and he quickly discerned that this man was most likely a hunter and trapper and posed no threat. He eased himself up onto his feet and stepped out into the open as he called out, "Hello friend. Come on in. Just being a little cautious until I had sized up who you are. Your pots gave you away."

The man turned and looked at LaBerge for a long moment and then said, "I understand. I'd have done the same."

LaBerge walked back to his camp and stood near the dead fire as the man rode on into the camp. He dismounted and stepped forward as he said, "Howdy, I'm Ephraim Sykes. I didn't expect to run into anyone up this way."

"I'm Jean LaBerge. You're moving about early in the day."

"Yes, I'm anxious to get back to my cabin. Been down to the settlement of Prestonsburg to lay in some supplies. I mostly hunt and trap in the mountains of these parts. Pushed my animals hard yesterday and decided to get an early start this morning. It was a hard night, what with the rain and all, I didn't sleep much."

"I'll get the fire up and going and we'll have some coffee," said LaBerge. "You had anything to eat this morning?"

"Nah, not much. Just chewed on some jerky."

"Find a dry spot, if you can, and make yourself comfortable. Once I get a fire up, I'll stir up a batch of biscuits and gravy."

"I appreciate it. Very thoughtful of you." Sykes brushed the water from a log and seated himself. He said nothing as he watched the tall man gather wood and get a fire going. The man went about his tasks with easy, efficient movements. He surmised that this was a man who was comfortable in his own skin, and a man who could take care of himself, even when cornered. As the fire began to pick up, Sykes said, "I'd guess from yer accent that yer not from around here. Am I right?"

"Yes, I'm from Vermont."

"The war's over with those Red Coats and I'd guess ya is headed west to stake a claim to some land." "Yeah, that's about it."
"Yer off the beaten path some. Most of the travelers avoid these parts. Too much up and down here in the mountains."

LaBerge didn't answer as he busied himself with preparing the biscuits and then he looked up at Sykes. "You ever hear of a place called the Roost? I've been told it's nearby and a hideout for a man named Belle Turk."

68

Instantly a startled look came to Sykes' face and Jean thought he could see a tightening of the man's muscles in his chest and arms as he said. "Yeah! And why would you want to have anything to do with Belle Turk and the Roost?"

LaBerge looked at Sykes. He was sure the man was what he claimed to be, a hunter and trapper. He'd come clean with him; perhaps he'd learn something from the trapper. "Some friends of mine have been abducted and taken to the Roost. If I can find it, I intend to rescue them. I've been told it's on the north side of Flag Knob Mountain. Is that right?"

Sykes said nothing for a long moment as he fumbled for a corncob pipe and a pack of tobacco. "You all alone in this plan to free your friends or have ya got help a comin'?"

"I'm alone. Do you know where it's located? I was told it was located up a sharp valley on this mountain, off of Wolf Creek."

"Yeah, I know where it is. Not sure I should tell ya. If ya go up there ya will most likely get yourself killed." He paused for a minute and then continued, "Yer too young to die, but I guess a man will do most anything to help his friends."

"Yes, he will. It's a young girl and her parents. Three men, led by a man named Kilkenny, have abducted them and taken them to the Roost."

Sykes stood to his feet and his face was now clouded as he said. "This man Kilkenny and his gang are a bad bunch and have quite a reputation. He preys on travelers that come through headed west. He'll be a tough nut for ya ta crack!"

"I figured as much from when I first met him, shortly after we left the flatboat at Huntington. What about this man, Belle Turk? What's his reputation? Worse than Kilkenny's?"

Sykes returned to his seat on the log. He said nothing for a long moment and then he spoke. "Kilkenny is the worst of the two. Turk and his men live outside the law, but they don't rob and steal from ordinary folks. Based on what I hear, Turk and his men mostly loaf and gamble. They've been accused of robbing a coach or a bank, but I know nothing for sure on that score."

"Well, thanks for the information. How do I find this place?"

Sykes smiled at LaBerge, but didn't answer his question as he said, "This girl. Does she mean anything special to you? Known her long, have ya?"

"No, not long. Met her and her parents on the flatboat coming down the Ohio."

"How do you know they have this girl? Were you there when they took her and her family?"

"No, but I got it out of the two men Kilkenny sent to get me. They told me Kilkenny was taking them to the hideout they called the Roost."

Sykes had to smile to himself. Based on what he had seen of the tall man over the past hour he wasn't surprised to hear that the two men had failed to capture him. "So, Kilkenny sent two men for you and ya outfoxed 'em? How'd ya do that?"

"Wasn't hard. I took care of one of the men and my dog handled the other man."

Jean filled a tin plate with biscuits and gravy and handed it to Sykes. "Thanks" he said. "Looks as if ya can also cook." He fell silent while he ate, and then looked across at LaBerge. "Yer goin' up against a stacked deck when ya get to the Roost. There'll likely be at least a half dozen men there. Don't seem to me ya got much of a chance of rescuing that girl and her parents against them odds. You'll likely get killed tryin'."

"Perhaps, but I'm going to try. I've faced heavy odds before."

Sykes sopped up some gravy with the edge of a biscuit as he grinned at LaBerge. "I'd guess ya were in the war and had a few run ins with the Red Coats."

"A few."

Sykes set his plate down, grabbed up a stick and began to draw lines in the wet dirt. "Look here," he said. "I'll show ya where the Roost is located. It's up a narrow valley off of Wolf Creek, high up on the north side of Flag Knob Mountain. I'd say about twenty miles from here. Head east from here until ya come to Wolf Creek, then go up the creek until ya come to the big beaver dam and then ya want to turn and head up the first valley to the right. Their hideout, which they call the Roost, is near the head of this valley. It's on the right side of the valley out on a high shelf. They've built several cabins for themselves. It's hard to get there without being spotted as they'll likely have lookouts posted."

"Yeah, I figured it wasn't going to be easy. I'll come up with something."

Sykes fell silent for a moment. "If I was wantin' ta get there without being seen, I'd try comin' in from above. From the shelf above ya can look down on the camp and get the lay of the land. From there it won't be easy to come down into the camp, but there is an old Indian trail down from the precipice. And I'd come in at night; that's your best bet and if yer careful you might get in undetected. It's up to you what ya do after that to rescue yer friends."

"I'll figure out a way, once I've got the lay of the hideout."

Sykes sopped up the last of his breakfast and then turned to his horse. "I best be on my way." He held out his hand. "Thanks for the breakfast." He patted his stomach. "The biscuits and gravy sure went down well." He held out his hand to LaBerge as he said, "And good luck! Yer gonna need all the luck ya can find ta rescue that girl and her parents. From what I hear, Kilkenny is a hard case. You'll most likely have to kill him to get to the girl!"

LaBerge watched Sykes as he rode away from his camp. Within a few minutes he was lost from his view. He looked up at the sky. The rain had stopped, and he could see small patches of blue in the western sky. It would be a nice day. He turned to packing his burro and saddled his horse. He now knew more details as to the general location of the Roost. His next challenge was getting in undetected. He'd find a way. He'd tackled tough fortifications before.

CHAPTER 9

Belle Turk

Is eyes narrowed, his face darkened, and his teeth clinched tight as he watched the oxen struggle to pull the wagon up the last few yards of the steep trail. Belle Turk stood at the window of his cabin, holding back the curtain with his hand, as he watched Kilkenny lash at the oxen with his whip and yell curses at the struggling animals. He continued to watch with raising anger as the harassed oxen slowly pulled the wagon up the last few yards of the steep trail and out onto the relatively level ground of the clearing that Turk called *The Roost*. He continued to watch with hard eyes as Kilkenny directed the oxen across the rocky shelf and brought them to a halt in front of a rough log cabin. Two men on horseback, that he recognized as Kilkenny's men, rode beside the wagon, and a man that was a stranger to him, walked beside the wagon.

Turk's anger continued to rise as Kilkenny stepped down from the wagon and began to unhitch the oxen. Turk uttered an oath to himself. *The man acted as if he owned the place! He hadn't even shown him the courtesy of coming to his cabin and requesting permission to stay overnight. Why had he come here?* He had a visceral dislike for Kilkenny, which had grown over several meetings. Turk thought of Kilkenny as a stubborn, vile, and uncouth man, utterly without principles, who preyed on the weak and unfortunate. The last time Kilkenny had been at the Roost he had suggested, in none too subtle language, that he and his men were not welcome to return. But despite this admonition, the man was back.

His eyes widened in surprise as the tail gate of the wagon came down with a jar and a young girl jumped to the ground. Within moments a woman appeared at the rear of the wagon and the unknown man and young girl helped her to the ground. The woman took a few halting steps, and he could readily see that she had injured her leg or ankle. "Damn!" he exclaimed. "Just what we need; two women and a strange man here at the Roost."

Turk turned his attention back to Kilkenny and one of his men, as they led the oxen away from the wagon and toward the rocky meadow where the horses and a few cows were pastured. His face darkened and he swore as he said to himself. *"He acts as if he intends to stay for a spell! More people to feed and more animals to eat up the grass!"* He turned from the window and walked toward the door. *Why had Kilkenny brought these people here?* He'd have it out with the man now, before they got settled in. He'd demand that Kilkenny and his entourage leave at daylight tomorrow. He wanted nothing to do with Kilkenny. Trouble followed the man like bears to honey.

Belle Turk was a big man of over six feet in height, with broad, heavy shoulders, short neck, and beefy arms and hands. He was dressed in heavy buckskin pants, tasseled shirt, and dark, heavy boots. As he walked towards the door of his cabin, he grabbed a large black three-cornered hat from a table and jammed it down hard onto his head. Turk was a man who lived along the edges of the law, but his clothing was tidy and free of soil and dirt. The Roost was his home and domain, and he resented the intrusion of Kilkenny and his entourage of people.

Hannah Cody's attention was immediately caught by the big man as he stepped from the log cabin and walked with wide steps toward Kilkenny who was returning from the meadow where he had taken the oxen. From the determined steps of the man, she surmised that he was upset about something. Another angry man frightened her, especially after what had happened last night with Kilkenny.

Her eyes quickly darted about the rocky enclave, taking in the several cabins and the horses, cows, and oxen grazing in the rocky meadow. She shifted her eyes back to the big man as he strode on toward Kilkenny and a shudder ran through her body. *They were prisoners at an isolated hideout, where there was almost no chance of their being found and rescued. What were they to do?*

In her distress, her thoughts turned to the tall, buckskin clad stranger, Jean LaBerge, who had befriended her father when he assisted him in loading the wagon onto the flatboat. When they were about to go their separate ways, he had warned her father about these rough men and her father had dismissed the danger. The danger had been real and now they were prisoners, and she had even been assaulted. As she thought of him, hope rose in her heart; perhaps he would come and rescue her and her parents. She shook her head; it was a foolish thought. And then she remembered his stolen kiss at the edge of the campsite and his request to come and see her at Olive Hill. She doubted if she would see him before then, and perhaps she would never see him again. He had promised to come, but something could come up that would prevent him from coming. He was handsome and strong and perhaps another woman would claim him before he could come to Olive Hill. Fear came again and gripped her heart. *Would she and her parents ever get to Olive Hill?*

In addition, the tall stranger was most likely unaware that she and her parents were being held as prisoners. She suddenly remembered the two men that Kilkenny had sent to rob him. These men had not returned. Unexpectedly, a new and sweet hope sprang up in her heart. Something had happened to thwart the men's plans to rob him. Perhaps he would learn of their plight and would, once again, come to the aid of her family. Yes, she was sure she knew the measure of the tall stranger. If he learned that they had been taken prisoner, he *would* come.

She shook all thoughts of the tall stranger from her mind as she turned her attention to her mother. Today's rough ride up the mountain had been even worse than yesterdays, and especially hard on her mother, who had been jostled and slammed from side to side as she rode in the wagon. She looked up to see Keaton as he strode across the enclave toward them.

When he drew near, he pointed to the rough log cabin that stood next to the wagon. It was built low, at little more than five feet high, with a dirt and grass covered roof. She could see two windows, although neither appeared to have any glass. Shabby strips of cloth hung from the windows, affording only a modicum of privacy. Keaton was at her side now as he pointed, "You folks will be staying in this cabin."

He pointed toward a log building that was a little larger than the other buildings, "That's the mess hall where we eat. Turks got a cook that fixes a couple of poor meals a day."

Keaton looked at Hannah for a moment, glanced about the rough yard, and then back at Mr. Cody. "The cabin ain't much and this is no place for you folks, but I guess you'll just have to make the best of it. Hope ya don't have ta stay here for too long." He turned to the wagon. "You let me know if I can help unload yer belongings."

Keaton turned and started to walk toward where Kilkenny and Turk were conversing in loud voices. After a few paces he halted and turned as he muttered to himself. *"Best to avoid that set-to. I can see Turk's riled about something.* He walked on toward a cabin that stood up against a rocky outcrop. Taggert had taken his horse to the cabin and was unloading his pack and removing the saddle. He glanced at Keaton as he approached, "It looks like Turk's got his dander up."

"Yeah, sure does."

Taggert glanced across to where the wagon stood, as he watched the man and the young girl assist the woman into the cabin. "I'd' guess Turk's out of sorts because we've returned here to the Roost when he told Kilkenny not to come back. And he's also probably upset that we brought those folks up here to the Roost." He looked back at Keaton. "No one is supposed to bring any strangers here to the hideout. If these folks leave here alive, they'll know where the Roost is located. It was dumb to bring 'em up here, but Kilkenny's got it in his head that Cody can get his hands on a wad of money. I hope he knows what he's doing, especially after attempting to assault the girl last night. It was a stupid thing to do and will only make things worse. Now that his daughter has been assaulted Cody may be unwilling to write for the money. It's a mess, that's what it is!"

With an oath, Keaton threw his saddle down beside the cabin as he continued, "We're in a box, Taggert, I don't hold with killin' women folk, and especially a young girl like her. I'll not stand by and see that happen!"

Taggert didn't reply for a moment and then said, "I agree, but what we gonna do if it comes ta that? Kilkenny's a tough and ruthless man. I'm not sure I want ta buck him. We'd most likely end up dead as mackerels with our throats slit. We'd both be better off if we had never hooked up with the man."

"Yer right, we never should have taken up with him. But sometimes ya do what ya gotta do to survive. I hope to get shut of him before too long, and I'll kill him if I have to! He's tough," said Keaton. "But a knife will cut him just like anyone else. The girl proved that last night! If he gets a knife stuck in him or a ball from my rifle in his gut, he'll bleed and die just like any man." He smiled a crooked smile as he continued. "That girl's got spunk. I'd never have guessed she carried a knife and knew how to use it. I sure don't plan on assaulting her. No sir!!"

He looked at Taggert with bold determination on his face as he said. "Kilkenny takes me for a milk sop, but I've been around the mountain a few times. He'll find out I'm no pushover if he backs me up again' a wall."

Taggert changed the subject as he said. Shad and Retford haven't come back. Kilkenny sent them to find that man, LaBerge, and get his money belt and anything else he had of value. I wonder what happened ta them?"

Keaton looked up from rubbing down his horse. "Those two guys are as dumb as rocks. I knew when they left that they'd never take that man, LaBerge. I sized that tall man up the evening we rode into their camp. He's been around the horn, and I'd guess was in the war. He ain't afraid of nothin' or nobody. I suspect he knows how ta handle himself. The guy may be young, but I'd guess he took out a few Red Coats during the war. An' he's got that dog a taggin' along with him." He looked up at Taggert, a broad grin across his face. "Ya never wants ta tangle with a man and his dog. If one doesn't get ya the other one will! I'd guess that between him and that dog those two guys never had a chance. Shad and Retford are either dead or ridin' hard ta save their hides."

"Yeah, I'd guess yer right. We'll likely never see Shad or Retford again. You suppose this guy LaBerge will come ta get the girl and her family?"

Keaton smiled up at Taggert, "I seen him eyein' the girl. Not with a bad eye, like Kilkenny, mind ya, but with care and concern in his eyes. If he learns they are being held here, he'll come. Ya can bet on it!" He grinned at Taggert. "I sort of hope he does come. It would save us a lot of grief."

Suddenly the attention of the two men was drawn to the loud voice of Belle Turk. Taggert and Keaton turned to see Kilkenny and Turk standing near the entrance to the main cabin where Turk lived when he was at the Roost. They could see that Turk's face was red with anger as he shouted, "I told you not to come back here to the Roost! And here ya have come back with two woman and a man. I won't stand for it. I want ya to pack up and get out of her at first light tomorrow morning. I want to be shut of ya. Yer nothing but trouble. Trouble hounds ya like fleas on a dog."

Kilkenny didn't flinch as he took a step closer to Turk. "Ah simmer down Turk. I didn't think ya meant we could never come back here to the Roost, and besides, this is important to me. I'm gonna make a lot of money off this man Cody." He took a step closer to Turk as he continued. "Why, I'll even give ya a cut."

Turk waved his hand, "I don't care about yer money or a cut of it. I want ya gone! That's what I want!"

Turk paused for a moment as he looked at Kilkenny's shirt. "There's blood on yer shirt! "What happened to ya? It looks like ya are all bandaged up underneath yer shirt."

Kilkenny glanced down at his side for a moment and then back up at Turk. "It's nothing," he said, "Just a bad cut along my side. I'll be as good as new in a few days."

Well, I don't give a damn about yer injury. I want ya to clear out of here by tomorrow."

Kilkenny stepped directly in front of Kirk as he yelled, "I'm not goin! I'll not leave until I'm good and ready ta leave!"

Taggart and Keaton watched with open mouths as the two men glared at each other as they stood almost toe to toe. Both had a pistol tucked into their belts, and for a moment Keaton feared that one of them would jerk out his gun and try and kill the other. He held his breath as he watched the men, and then slowly Kilkenny took a step back and then turned and walked away from Turk, almost daring him to shoot him in the back.

Turk watched Kilkenny's back for a long moment. *Damn the man!* He was still as stubborn and obstinate as ever. For a brief moment he considered jerking out his gun and shooting the troublemaker in the back. He'd killed a couple of men but shooting a man in the back wasn't to his liking. He was mad, but he'd wait. There would come a time of reckoning. He was sure of it. As he watched Kilkenny walk into his cabin and shut the door a sixth sense told him that he hadn't heard the truth about the wound on the man's side.

Taggert let out a low whistle as he watched the door to Kilkenny's cabin shut. "That was close!" he ejaculated. "I doubt if those two men can live together here in the Roost for long. One of them is gonna die if we stay here."

Hannah and her father helped her mother to the door of the cabin. They stopped at the open door and her father said, "Wait here while I check it out. I hope there's a cot where your mother can lie down." Within a few minutes he walked back out and said, "It's

78

rough, with only a dirt floor, but there are three cots." He looked at his wife. "Come, Cathedra, Hannah and I will help you to a cot where you can get off that bum ankle and rest a bit, after that hard ride up the mountain."

They led Cathedra into the cabin and helped her lie down on a cot. Hannah removed her mother's shoes and when she looked about the cabin, she found a tattered blanket that was lying on a shelf. She shook out the blanket and then covered her mother. "There, that will help to keep you comfortable," she said.

Cathedra looked up at her daughter as she said, "Thank you Hannah. You are such a wonderful daughter." She glanced up at her husband. "Jedidiah were in a mess!" Cathedra looked up at her husband, her face filled with pain and worry, as she continued, "Jedidiah, what are you going to do to get us away from here and out of the clutches of these evil men? And, after what happened last night, you must protect our daughter."

Hannah's father said nothing for a long moment as he looked down at his wife, and his voice was barely above a whisper as he said, "I . . . I don't know Mother. I'll try and think of something." He glanced at Hannah and then said, "But I *will* protect my daughter, even if it kills me."

Mrs. Cody reached up and took her husband's hand in hers. "I . . . I don't mean to scold, Jedidiah, but you should have listened to that tall stranger when he said to be wary of these men. If you had listened to him, we wouldn't be on this terrible fix!"

"Yes, I made a mistake. We should have stayed with the other wagons and not gone off by ourselves. They were waiting for just such an opportunity to pounce." He glanced at Hannah as he continued, "I've bought us some time, telling Kilkenny that all our money is back in New York. I'll try and make the best of it."

Hannah interrupted her father, "But Pa, There's no money back in New York! It's all out there in the floor of the wagon!"

"Yeah, but Kilkenny doesn't know that. I'm hoping that someone will rescue us before Kilkenny learns the truth."

"Who?" interjected Mrs. Cody from the cot. "Nobody even knows we're here in this hidcout."

Cody reached and took his wife's hand as he said, "I don't know, Mother. I'm just praying that someone will come and help us."

On an impulse Hannah spoke, "I'm going to try and escape and see if I can find help."

Her mother looked up at her, a startled look on her face as she exclaimed, "Oh Hannah, you can't do that! It's far too dangerous."

"Perhaps, but I'm going to try. Not tonight. I'll wait for a few days until I see how they operate this hideout and if they have a watch out during the night."

Cody looked at Hannah, loving concern written across his face as he said, "It's very dangerous for you, but I'll try and help you get away."

CHAPTER 10

Grace Growden Galloway

J ames Patterson reined in his horse as he turned and spoke to the woman that rode at his side, "We'll halt here by the spring and take our mid-day meal before pushing on. I trust that is satisfactory with you Ma'am. I'm sure you will welcome a respite from riding."

She looked across at him, a look of weariness and determination on her face as she said, "Yes, let's stop for a spell. I'm somewhat fatigued."

Patterson quickly dismounted and then assisted the woman from her horse. He led her to a small boulder that lay next to the stream and was about to help her to take a seat on the rock when she said, "No, James, I'll stand for a bit before I set down. In fact, I think I'll walk about and stretch my legs for a few minutes. I'm not used to these long horseback rides."

"Yes Ma'am, that's an excellent idea," replied James. "You take a little walk while I rustle us up something to eat." He glanced along the stream. "Do be careful Ma'am; the grounds rough and you could easily trip and fall."

"Yes, I'll be careful. I wouldn't want to injure myself, especially in this remote area."

As he turned from her, he said, "I'm sorry Ma'am, the food won't be up to the fine cooking you are accustomed to, or even the meals we've been taking at the inn." He paused for a moment and his face was filled with a deferential question as he said, "Perhaps we should have stayed on at the inn for a few more days, instead of pushing on into these desolate mountains?"

The woman looked up at him as she rubbed the small of her back. "Whatever you prepare for us to eat will do very nicely, James. And I felt that we had to leave the inn. If we had stayed on, I feel quite sure that man, Swingate Calvert, would have found us. I must get away from him. I'll never sign the deeds to my property, and I may be able to escape him by leaving the inn and traveling on through these rough mountains towards my sister's home. Perhaps the roughness of the mountains will discourage him from pursuing me further."

"Yes, I understand Ma'am. However, I fear that we may become lost here in this wilderness and I believe it is still some considerable distance to the settlement where your sister resides, if we can be so lucky as to locate it Since we left traveling by coach and along the roads, such as they were, and struck out across these infernal mountains it's been hard going, especially for you Ma'am."

"Never mind the hardships, James, and the possibility of getting lost. I have every confidence we will be able to make our way to my sister's home, and hopefully, we will elude that persistent man."

"Yes Ma'am, I will do my best."

"Yes, James, I know you will. You have been most faithful to me during these very trying years of the Rebel rebellion against the King, and the loss of my husband, daughter, and property." She gave a sigh, and her face was grim, and her voice filled with sadness as she looked at James. "The Rebels have been victorious, and I am in a very weak position. Nevertheless, I pray that I will someday be able to regain my property and to properly compensate you for your loyal service."

"Yes Ma'am, but now is not the time to be worrying about payment for my services. That will come later. I'll get a fire going and see what I can warm up for us to eat."

"Thank you, James." Grace Growden Galloway lifted her billowing long skirt to just above her ankles as she walked along the stream, being careful to avoid any rocks or stones that might cause her to trip and fall. She walked for a short distance, as she stretched her back and legs, in an attempt to relieve some of the ache. She was not accustomed to riding long distances, sidesaddle on a horse, along poor trails and through rough mountains. It was, indeed, a considerable change from her earlier years of wealth and comfort.

She had grown up in eastern Pennsylvania, the daughter of Lawrence Growden, a wealthy owner of the Growden Iron Furnace Company and a member of the Pennsylvania Assembly. They had lived in a large mansion and rode about, to church, and to visit friends, in an elegant four-wheeled coach, driven by a coachman and pulled by four white horses. Her heart was heavy with pain and sadness as she thought of her husband, Joseph Galloway, and her daughter, Betsy. It had been five years since her husband and daughter had fled to England to escape the wrath of the Rebels led by George Washington, and the multitude of men who were engaged in the rebellion against the Crown. She had to struggle to hold back the tears as she walked along the stream. She would never see her husband and daughter again. They had both died when a plague of cholera had swept through London. It seemed that disaster had stalked her like a hungry wolf. It had been several years now since the Executive Council had taken her property from her and this man, Swingate Calvert, who had purchased the property from the Council, was now hounding her to sign the deeds which would complete the sale of the property to Calvert and make it legal. Despite her present poor circumstances, she still maintained her pride and self-esteem, and she was determined to never sign the deeds; she would die first.

She and her husband had not supported the rebellion against King George and the Crown, and along with others, had remained steadfast in their loyalty to the King. That loyalty was the root cause of all of her burdens and problems. The Rebels called her and her husband by a variety of names, *Loyalist, Royalists, King's Men, and Tories.* She preferred to be called a Loyalist, as she viewed herself as being a loyal follower of good King George.

The idea of the colonies breaking away from England, and forming their own government and country, had always been abhorrent to her and her husband. When her husband and daughter had fled to England to escape the wrath of the Rebels, she had remained at their mansion, supervising their various properties and business enterprises. Her husband had taken their daughter, Betsy, along as company. She had remained behind to look after their property as they had thought it unlikely the Rebels would harm a woman or confiscate her property, much of which she had inherited from her father. None of the property was actually in her name, due to the law of *feme covert*. This law said that the legal rights of married women were absorbed by those of her husband. When the Rebels had gained power, the Executive Council had forceable evicted her from her home and all of the property that she and her husband owned. She had been left nearly penniless and had been forced to live in a rundown boarding house.

Their property had been sold to Mr. Swingate Calvert, but due to the death of her husband in England, her signature was required on the deeds to make the transaction binding and legal. She was determined to never sign the deeds and she was committed to every means at her disposal to regain her property. She was a determined and strong-willed woman and would never give up her quest to regain what she believed was rightfully hers.

She heard the voice of James as he called, "Come Ma'am. I've fixed a bite of food for the two of us."

She turned and walked back to the fire that James had built and seated herself on a fallen log. James handed her a tin plate, which held a cold sandwich and a small bowl of stew he had heated on the fire. "It's not much Ma'am," he said, "But I hope it will dull your hunger?"

"Yes, this will do very nicely James. You are most kind and helpful."

James helped himself to a sandwich and a bowl of the stew and then fell to eating. A half hour later James helped her up onto her horse and then mounted his horse. "We'll go along slow, Ma'am," he said. "Perhaps that will make things a bit easier for you?"

"Yes, I'm sure it will." She looked at him and tried to smile as she said, "I hope that we can make it to Pikeville before dark as I believe there is an inn there, where we can spend the night. It will likely be small and cramped, but it will be shelter."

"Yes, hopefully we can make it to the inn before dark," replied James. "I'd hate for you to have to spend the night in the open mountains and subject to the elements."

As James turned his horse to leave the stream, he was startled to see two men ride out from the cover of a grove of trees. As the men rode toward them James noted their dirty and unshaven condition and that one of the men held a long rifle in his hands, which appeared to be pointed directly toward him. James had seen the likes of these type of men before. They were most likely "road agents" intent on stealing their belongings, or worse. He quickly turned to Mrs. Galloway as he said in a low voice, "Hold on Ma'am, I don't like the looks of these men."

The two men rode their horses on toward James and Mrs. Galloway until they were only a few paces away and then pulled their mounts to a halt. The man, who did not appear to have a weapon, stared at the man and woman for a long moment, and then glanced at his companion as he muttered in a low voice, "Well Retford, it looks as if we've stumbled onto a couple of pigeons here."

Retford snickered, "Yes, I believe yer right, Shad. This may prove to be interesting, and profitable."

The man called Shad sat silent for a moment and then he said to his companion, "Let's see what they're carryin.' Probably won't be much, but I see the woman has a right smart broach about her neck." A smirk filled his face. "And she may have some money in her bag."

James drew himself up to his full height, as he stood forward in the stirrups of his saddle. His voice was firm, and he tried to fill it with authority as he called out, "You men be off and on your way. I'll not allow you to inconvenience Mrs. Galloway. We've no business with the likes of you."

Shad snickered as he turned to Retford. "Did ya hear that! We've got a tough guy on our hands. Ha! Ha! I'm near scared out of my wits!"

The two men slowly dismounted from their horses, stepped forward a few paces, and stopped. They stood, looking up at James and Mrs. Galloway with hard eyes and then Shad said, "That's a right nice-lookin' broach ya are wearin' ma'am. May I see it?"

Mrs. Galloway pulled lightly on the reins of her horse and the horse backed up a few steps as she said, "Certainly not! You men had best be on your way and leave us be."

James quickly reached down and grabbed the hatchet he always carried, from the scabbard strapped to his saddle. He swung down from the horse and stepped forward toward the two men, as he said, "You men get back on your horses and leave immediately. I'll not allow you to intimidate Mrs. Galloway and you certainly may not inspect her broach."

Retford took a step forward as he swung the long rifle up. "You shut up, old man! We just want a look at the woman's broach. Nothin' wrong with that!"

James raised his hatchet as he stepped forward. "No, you will not bother Mrs. Galloway. Now be off with . . ."

The explosion of the long rifle shattered the quiet of the green mountainside. The shock of the ball hitting his chest slammed James back and he fell hard to the ground. Mrs. Galloway screamed as she tried desperately to turn her horse away from Shad, as he grabbed for her horse's reins.

CHAPTER 11

The Rescue

Whenthe gunshot shattered the quiet harmony of the blue mountains, and reverberated through the trees and across the meadow, a covey of quail abandoned their pecking for seeds and rose into the sky in frantic flight. A deer. that had been feeding along the edge of a nearby meadow, turned sharply and bound into the safety of the timber, his tail held high. Jean LaBerge's horse instinctively shied hard to the left, and the dog, Shag, whirled and growled, his ears turned sharply forward as he stared in the direction of the sharp sound.

LaBerge gave a sharp tug on the reins of his horse as he quickly brought him to a halt. He patted the horse on the neck as he said in a low voice, "Take it easy boy." He had turned to look down at the dog when he heard a woman's shrill scream.

The tall man was a man of action, and he instantly jerked his horse to the right toward the direction of the gunshot and scream and dug his spurs sharply into the horse's flanks. Seeing this action, the dog growled again and began to run hard ahead of the horse. Within a few moments LaBerge and the dog burst into a small clearing that bordered Wolf Creek. LaBerge saw a finely dressed woman, who sat side-saddle on an Appaloosa horse as she tugged franticly at the reins of her horse in a futile effort to pull the horse free from a man who had a tight grasp on the horse's bridle.

"Let go of my horse, you scoundrel!" she exclaimed in a shrill voice.

Nearby, a man stood, with a long rifle in his hand, as he looked down on a man who lay in the grass, clutching his chest and shoulder, his face grimaced in pain.

LaBerge instantly recognized the two men as the same men who had tried to rob him two days before. Anger swelled up in him as he pointed at the man holding the gun and yelled at the dog, "Get him Shag!" The dog was off like a ball fired from a rifle; his mouth wide open and yapping loudly as he charged the man, who immediately dropped his rifle and began to run franticly towards the creek.

In the same instant LaBerge directed his horse toward the man who had a grip on the bridle of the woman's horse. The man's eyes were suddenly filled with fear and alarm as the big horse bore down on him. He quickly lost interest in the woman, and her broach, as he released his grasp on the bridle. turned and began to run toward the trees along the creek. Within moments LaBerge's horse caught the man from behind and sent him sprawling to the ground. LaBerge was off his horse in an instant.

Jean LaBerge was a big man with strong shoulders and arms, the result of hard work on a rocky Vermont farm, and he didn't hold back as he hit the man full in the face with two hard blows. The man slumped to the ground, as blood spurted from his face and nose. He groaned as he tried to regain his feet and then fell back to the ground. LaBerge looked down at him as he said, "Stay down or I'll give you some more."

Laberge quickly ran to the woman's frightened horse and grabbed the bridle. He patted the horse on the neck as he said in soothing tones, "Whoa boy, everything is alright now."

He looked up at the woman. "I'll help you down Ma'am." She held out her arms and he quickly helped her to the ground. He handed the reins of the horse to her as he said, "Hold these while I tend to the other man."

When he turned, he wasn't surprised at what he saw, as the snarling of the dog, Shag, and the man's grunts, yells, and curses filled the little meadow. A couple of hundred feet away the man lay sprawled on the ground, his legs and arms churning in a futile effort to fight off the snarling dog and protect his face. The man with the injured shoulder had managed to rise to his knees and was urging the dog on as he yelled, "Atta boy! Eat him up!"

LaBerge stepped to the dog and man. "Okay Shag, that's enough. Let him be." Reluctantly the dog backed away but continued to stand nearby; his teeth barred and low growls coming from his throat.

LaBerge looked down at the man. "Don't move! You stay where you are or I'll sic the dog back on you, and I may not call him off if I have to do it again."

LaBerge turned and knelt beside the injured man who was struggling to get to his feet. LaBerge could see blood flowing from a wound to his upper right chest and shoulder. "Rest easy mister," he said, "I've got a kit in my saddle bag. Sit back down and I'll see what I can do for that gunshot wound."

The man looked up at LaBerge, his breathing hard and his eyes filed with pain. "I'm much obliged mister, but first take a look at Mrs. Galloway and make sure she's okay."

Mrs. Galloway had calmed her horse and the two of them now stood beside LaBerge as she looked down at the man with the wounded shoulder. "I'm fine James," she said. "There is no need to worry about me, thanks to the intervention of this brave young man."

LaBerge extended his hand to the lady as he said, "I'm Jean LaBerge. I'm sorry we've met under such trying circumstances."

She shook his hand vigorously, for a woman, as she looked up at him. Her smile was firm as she looked directly into his eyes. He immediately formed the opinion that this was a woman who was accustomed to giving orders and expecting obedience and respect in return. She spoke with a firm voice, "I'm Grace Growden Galloway." She glanced down at the injured man as she continued, "And this is

James Patterson, my assistant. Please accept my sincere thanks for coming to our aid against these ruffians. I can see that you are a man of action and integrity."

"It was my pleasure Ma'am. I'm happy that I was close by when I heard the gunshot and your scream."

"Yes . . . yes that was most fortunate."

She was about to turn back to James when he said, "Ma'am would you be related to the Mr. Growden who owned the Growden Iron Furnace Company and was a member of the Pennsylvania Assembly?"

She turned back to him. "Yes, I was his daughter. My father is deceased, and my husband and I operated the furnace company, and other properties, until we lost everything during the late war of independence." She paused for a long moment as she appraised him with her eyes. And then continued, "Mr. LaBerge, I strongly suspect we were on opposite sides during the war, as my husband and I remained loyal to the King and opposed the war for independence from England."

"Yes, I was an officer in the army and served under General Washington. So, we were, indeed, on opposite sides, but that is of no consequence now. The war is over, and I am pleased that I could be of assistance to you today."

"Yes, we can be friends now, and I thank you again for your assistance in rescuing myself and James from these men who were intent on robbing us, or worse. She looked down at James Patterson. "Enough of this talk." She quickly knelt and pulled open James' shirt. "It's a nasty wound," she exclaimed. "We must get you to a doctor."

She stood to her feet as she said to LaBerge. "I'll get some water from the stream while you get your kit. We'll cleanse his wound and perhaps that will give him a measure of relief, but we must get him to a doctor as soon as possible!"

LaBerge retrieved his kit from his saddle bag and then returned to James. Within moments Mrs. Galloway returned with a small basin of water, a towel, and some cloths. "I'll tend to James' wound," she said.

She glanced at the two men and then at LaBerge. "I suggest you restrain those men in some fashion. They are scoundrels, and I don't trust them, even with the dog watching them."

"Yes Ma'am," he said. LaBerge stepped to the nearest man, who was now setting up and was attempting to wipe the blood from his face with the tattered sleeve of his shirt. Shag crouched nearby, as he continued to bare his teeth and growl. LaBerge looked down at the man and quickly recognized him as the same man his dog had attacked two days ago. He suppressed a smile as he said, "You're a slow learner! In addition, you don't follow orders very well. Get to your feet!"

When the man had struggled to his feet, LaBerge shoved him toward his partner, who continued to sit on the ground as he wiped the blood from his face with a rag he had pulled from his pocket. LaBerge whistled to his horse, who immediately trotted to his side. He quickly retrieved some rawhide from his saddle bag and then bound the hands of the two men behind their backs. He stepped away and looked down at the men. "You're both as dumb as rocks!" he exclaimed. "Two days ago, I gave you your horses and a rifle, and told the two of you to ride north and leave the country. Instead, you were riding to the Roost and have attempted to rob this man and woman. I'll not give you a second chance to ride away." The two men said nothing as they stared up at LaBerge with questioning and fear filled eyes.

LaBerge turned to his dog. "Watch them Shag," He returned to where the woman continued to kneel at the side of the man. "How's it going Ma'am," he said. "Can I help?"

She looked up at him. "I've cleansed the wound, but the ball needs to come out. We must get him to a doctor before nightfall." She stood to her feet. "I believe there is a doctor in Williamson, on the Big Sandy River, where we stayed last night. If we leave immediately, we can probably make it back there before night fall. Thank goodness the sun sets late during this time of year."

LaBerge started to say that he couldn't go to Williamson, as he was on another important mission, and then stopped. He had no choice; he must assist this lady and her injured servant. In addition, the two men who had attempted to rob Mrs. Galloway and James, and had shot James, must be turned over to the authorities. He wasn't going to make the mistake of turning them loose again. "Yes, we'll leave immediately. Do you know if there is a sheriff in Williamson?"

She fell silent for a moment. "I can't rightly say for sure, but I think it likely." She glanced at the two men who were seated on the ground with their hands tied behind their backs. "I take it you're planning to take these two scoundrels along and turn them over to the law?"

"Yes, that's my intention."

"Good! They'll slow us down a mite, but not much. Let's get James on his horse and be on our way. Times a wasting."

LaBerge walked to where the man had dropped the long rifle, when his dog had attacked him, and picked it up. He inspected it to make sure it wasn't primed and then tied it to his saddle. He gathered the two men's horses and led them to where the men were seated. "Mount up," he said. "We're going to Williamson on the Big Sandy River. I'm going to turn you men over to the Sheriff there. He paused as he looked down at the two men. "I want you men to understand me! I'll come down hard on any attempt to escape, or an act of violence or resistance. When my dog and I are finished with you, you'll wish you were dead. In addition, I'll carry through with my earlier threat to turn you out in this wilderness in your socks without your horses, your canteens, or a rifle."

LaBerge turned from the two men and looked across at the woman and man. With the help of Mrs. Galloway, James had struggled to his feet. The two men's hands were tied behind their backs, so LaBerge helped the men mount their horses and then he led their horses to where the man and woman were standing. LaBerge helped James mount his horse and then assisted Mrs. Galloway onto her horse.

Within a few minutes they rode away from Wolf Creek and the meadow. Mrs. Galloway led the way, followed by the two men, who were shadowed by the dog as he continued to growl in low tones. LaBerge and James brought up the rear of the party. LaBerge rode at James' side, his arm encircling his waist to steady him and make sure he didn't slip from the saddle.

The sun had set, and deep twilight had fallen as they rode into the settlement of Williamson. They were tired and worn, and James, his shirt red with blood, was leaning heavily on LaBerge's arm and shoulder as they rode into the settlement.

Mrs. Galloway led the party to the rough log building which served as the inn and tavern. Before LaBerge could dismount to assist her, she had slid from her horse and entered the building to inquire as to rooms and a doctor. LaBerge quickly dismounted and helped James from his horse. He ordered the two men to dismount and to take chairs at a small table that stood near the entrance to the inn. He looked at Shag as he said, "Watch them boy. If they move, jump them." The dog immediately crouched in front of the two men, bared his teeth and began to growl.

Laberge assisted James into the inn and helped him to a chair at a small table, where he slumped forward onto the table. Within moments Mrs. Galloway was at the table. "The owner of the inn has sent a young boy to fetch the doctor." She glanced at LaBerge, "Let's get James to one of the two rooms I've taken, where he can lay down on a bed. I'm sure he's about all done in."

Within a few minutes James was stretched out on a cot. Mrs. Galloway looked down at him. "The doctor will be here shortly. I'll get you a cup of water while we wait for the doctor to arrive."

She turned to LaBerge, "The inn keeper says there's a sheriff here in Williamson. I suggest you get directions from him and then take those two ruffians to the sheriff. I assume they have a jail of some sort, or perhaps stocks." She looked up at LaBerge a slight grin on her face, "A few days in the stocks, without water or bread, might change their attitude some!"

LaBerge had to stifle a smile. He could readily see that Mrs. Galloway was accustomed to making decisions and giving orders and directions to others. "Yes, I'll take the two men to the sheriff and give him a full report on what they've done, including the wounding of James."

She looked up at Laberge. "Yes, I want those ruffians incarcerated for a good spell. They had no call to shoot James; he was only attempting to protect me!"

He secured directions from the inn keeper and then walked the two men the short distance to the small building that served as the office, jail, and apparently the home, of the sheriff. Shag tagged along behind LaBerge as they made their way through the deepening gloom of a cloudless night. LaBerge hammered on the door, and it was soon opened by a tall, middle-aged man dressed in rough buckskin, who looked at LaBerge with dark eyes. LaBerge gave the sheriff an accounting of the attack upon the woman and man and the shooting of James by the two men. "The man is seriously wounded, and we wish to press charges against these two men. Is there a Circuit Judge that can try these men?"

The tall sheriff said nothing as he stepped from the building and surveyed the two men for a long moment. He glanced at the dog and then grinned at LaBerge. "It looks as if one of these men has tangled with yer dog?"

"Yes, the dog helped me capture them."

The sheriff snickered as he looked back at the two men and then at LaBerge. "A dog is a man's best friend, or enemy," he exclaimed, "It all depends on which side of the dog yer on. Ha! Ha!"

The sheriff turned to the two men. "Get a move on into my office. The jail's in back and it'll hold ya until the judge comes by." He laughed a hearty laugh, as he said, "An don't try any funny stuff or I'll sic this man's dog on ya. Ha! Ha!"

The sheriff ceased his jesting and turned to LaBerge. "Yer in luck. The circuit judge comes through tomorrow. He holds his court here at my jail. Usually gets started at about eleven o'clock. You come back then and tell yer story to the judge."

"Yes, Mrs. Galloway and I will return then." LaBerge watched as the sheriff pushed the men into the building and then turned and walked back to the inn. He made his way to the small room where he had left Mrs. Galloway and James. Mrs. Galloway met him at the door of the room. "The doctor is administering a pain medication to James and will then remove the ball from his wound. He has a young man who is assisting him. There is little we can do here for now. I suggest we find a table and see if we can get something to eat."

They found seats at a table and a young lady soon appeared and asked them what they would like to eat. "You can choose between a venison steak or lamb chops. Take yer pick. Either one comes with fried potatoes and a bottle of ale."

They both ordered lamb. "It'll be ready in a half hour," exclaimed the young waitress.

Mrs. Galloway leaned back in her chair and gave a sigh. "I'm nearly worn to a frazzle. It's been a very long day with no progress, since I'm back where I began the day, here in Williamson."

"I'm sorry, Mrs. Galloway. I hope you . . ."

"How fortunate to find you here in the inn Mrs. Galloway." The interruption to their conversation came from a short, but heavy, man who had suddenly appeared at their table. He had broad shoulders and a round pudgy face, which carried dark heavy sideburns that ran down the sides of his face. His boots were black, and he was dressed in black, broadcloth pants and coat and a dark, grey trimmed, tricorne hat, all sober and expensive apparel. His eyes seemed to bulge from his face as he looked down at Mrs. Galloway. "I just arrived myself, only a few hours ago and I was hoping I would find you here." He paused as he looked down at her, a sly grin on his face. "I had almost gained the impression, Ma'am, that you were trying to evade me!"

Mrs. Galloway stared up at the man and LaBerge could see that her eyes were filled with loathing and anger, but she said nothing as he continued, "But, of course, as a lady of refinement, you would

95

never attempt to evade your lawful obligations." A laugh shook his ample body, "Obviously it was a foolish thought on my part to even consider such a possibility. Yes . . . yes, I was mistaken, and I'm sure it has all been an unfortunate misunderstanding that can be easily cleared up and put behind us." He patted the breast of his coat as he said, "I have the deeds here in my pocket and it won't take but a moment for you to sign the documents, in the presence of a witness, and then I can be on . . ."

Mrs. Galloway's eyes were now filled with anger and disgust as she found her voice; "I'll sign nothing Mr. Calvert! You are part of this evil plot to take my property from me and I'll have nothing to do with you." She waved her hand as she said, "Now be off with you and leave me alone."

The man's shaggy eyebrows lifted, and his face took on an instant hardness as he backed a step away from the table. His fat round face took on a shade of red and his voice was now filled with an ominous tone as he said, "You have no choice in the matter, Mrs. Galloway. The law says that you must sign deeds following the sale of the property to me. I insist that you sign, or I shall be forced to take the necessary legal steps to compel your compliance with the law."

Mrs. Galloway pushed her chair back a few inches from the table as she turned and looked up at the pudgy man. LaBerge could see the anger and determination in her face as she said. "I don't care a whit what the law says. I am of the strong opinion that my property was taken from me unlawfully and I will never sign the deeds. I'll go to prison before I sign those deeds, giving you, my property."

The pudgy man seemed to be at a loss for words for a brief moment as he stared down at her, a look of disbelief on his face. He stepped forward to within a foot of Mrs. Galloway and his voice was filled with harshness as he said, "You're making a big mistake Ma'am, I'll . . ."

Mrs. Galloway turned back to the table as she said, "Leave me be, Mr. Calvert. I do not wish to discuss the matter further. You might as well return to your home. You are wasting your time here."

Calvert said nothing for a long moment and when he spoke his voice was filled with anger and frustration as he said, "You leave me no choice, Ma'am. I'll . . . I'll go to the authorities and have you arrested."

She waved her hand. "Be gone, I'll not discuss the matter further with you."

Calvert seemed immobile, as if his feet were nailed to the floor, as he stared down at her with hard and angry eyes. His face was now filled with venom as he replied in a loud voice that carried across the small tavern. "You are a stubborn old woman, as well as a traitor, and you deserve to rot in prison! The Counsel took your property because you and your husband were turncoats who supported that evil King George against the cause of independence. I'll see that you rot in . . ."

LaBerge pushed back from the table and stood to his feet as he said, "You heard the lady, mister. Now make yourself scarce!"

At the sound of LaBerge's voice Calvert stepped back away from the table, as he seemed to take notice of LaBerge for the first time. He had a surprised look on his face as he said, "And who are you to be ordering me about?"

LaBerge stepped around the table and stood in front of the man as he said, "Let's just say I'm a friend of the lady and I'll not stand by and see her intimidated and threatened by you, or anyone else. Now leave her be, or I'll personally escort you out of the Inn."

A faint smile came across the man's face as he cast a quick glance about the little room, which held only a few patrons who had ceased eating their meal or drinking their ale to watch the unfolding confrontation at the table. Calvert snickered as he looked at LaBerge and ran his eyes up and down his tall frame, as if he were sizing him up. and then he exclaimed, "You and who else are going to throw me out!"

"I won't need any help," said LaBerge in a calm voice. He glanced down at his dog, who lay just under the table, as he continued,

97

"And if I do need any assistance, my dog, Shag, will be happy to assist me. He'd most likely enjoy chewing on some of that fat."

Calvert stepped back and looked down at the dog for a long moment. The dog sensed that he was being watched and he slowly raised his head and emitted a low growl. Calvert's eyes shifted from the dog and back to LaBerge. He said nothing for a moment as he cast his eyes across his antagonist again, and then he said, "You don't look the part, but you must be a turncoat, the same as this woman. You're both traitors, that's what you are!"

LaBerge's voice remained calm as he said, "You are mistaken. I served with General Washington's army. Don't call me a traitor again, or I'll not only escort you from the tavern but rough you up a bit while I'm about it."

Calvert's eyes widened as his eyes darted about the room for a long moment. He quickly discerned that it was unlikely that anyone would come to his aid against this man and his dog. He turned back to stare at LaBerge for a long moment as he slowly backed away a few steps and then he said, "If you served under General Washington during the war of independence then why are you coming to the aid of this traitorous woman?"

LaBerge's voice had now taken on an edge as he said, "For a couple of reasons: First, I don't like to see a woman being badgered by a man into doing something she doesn't want to do. And second, the war is over, and a peace treaty has been signed with the British." LaBerge stepped forward toward Calvert as he continued, "In fact, now that the Treaty of Paris has been signed, there is talk that property taken from the Loyalist's should be restored to them." He paused for a moment, as he continued to hold Calvert in his steady gaze. "I suspect that you know this and that is why you are pursuing Mrs. Galloway to get her to sign the deed before her property is returned to her. You're a despicable man Calvert. Now get out of the tavern and be on your way. If I see you again, I may not be able to restrain myself from rearranging your face a bit."

Calvert said nothing as he stared at LaBerge for a long moment and then he turned to Mrs. Galloway as he found his voice again. "I see you have hired protection to allow you to evade signing the deeds." He fell silent for a moment and then said, "I'll be leaving now, but you haven't heard the last of this matter, I'll be back." He took one last look at LaBerge and a quick glance down at the dog and then turned and stomped out of the tavern.

LaBerge returned to his chair at the table. He looked across the table at Mrs. Galloway. "Ma'am. I'd take what the man said seriously. I'm of the opinion that he'll be back and will continue to cause you trouble."

"Yes, I'm afraid you are most likely correct." She looked across the table at him, her face filled with questions and concern. "Mr. LaBerge, I've been running from this man for weeks. And now, with James injured, I'm at my wits end. I'm not sure what I can do."

"Do you have friends you can go to when James is able to travel? Someone who can give you, and James, some protection and assistance?"

"No, I'm essentially without friends." She paused as she cleared her throat. "As you heard Calvert say, I'm a Loyalist. My husband and I remained faithful supporters of King George during the war, and as Calvert said, the Counsel took all of our property. My husband is now dead, and I'm being hounded to sign these deeds, which will make it impossible for me to ever recover my property."

Mrs. Galloway looked across the table at LaBerge with searching and fear filled eyes. "Mr. LaBerge, I don't know what to do. James has been shot, and I believe seriously injured, and, as you just said, this man will most likely continue to hound me." She fell silent as she looked down at her plate for a long moment and then she slowly lifted her head as she looked at him with pleading eyes. "Will you help me Mr. LaBerge? Will you please help me?"

The fear in her eyes, and her choked and plaintive plea for help threw LaBerge into a quandary that tugged and pulled him in divergent directions. "I . . . I don't know if I can," he stammered. He fell silent for a long moment as turmoil raged in his heart. Two women; the beautiful Hannah Cody and the sophisticated Mrs.

Galloway, had unexpectedly interrupted his journey to Blue Valley, and both had pressing needs that it appeared only he could satisfy.

But within moments his active mind began to clear and the indecision to leave him. It was part of his upbringing: you did what you had to do, and without complaint or shirking. You hit the problem head on. He looked across the table at Mrs. Galloway and the hesitancy was gone, and his voice was now firm, as he said, "Mrs. Galloway, I must leave immediately to go and rescue a young lady and her family, which have been abducted. I'll most likely be gone for several days, perhaps a week, but if I'm delayed in returning, don't despair, I *will* return, and will then escort you and James to your final destination. You can count on it."

A smile came immediately to Mrs. Galloway's face as she looked across the table at him and spoke with a soft voice. "Thank you, Mr. LaBerge. You are a very kind and understanding gentleman." She reached and placed her hand on his arm as she looked up at LaBerge. "Please tell me about this young lady and why it is that she is being held against her will."

Over the course of the next few minutes LaBerge told Mrs. Galloway of meeting Hannah Cody on the flatboat, of the five men who had rode into the camp after they had left the boat, of the attempt by the two men, who were now being held by the sheriff in his jail, to rob him, and what he had learned from the two men as to the abduction of Hannah and her family. He ended his dissertation by exclaiming, "Hannah and her parents are apparently being held at a hideout called the Roost. I must go and rescue them."

"Oh dear!" exclaimed Mrs. Galloway as fear returned to her eyes. "Mr. LaBerge please do be careful in your quest to rescue this young lady and her parents. I surmise that this is most assuredly a dangerous mission you are about to undertake. I would be most distressed to learn that you had been injured, or killed, while attempting to rescue this young lady and her family. I shall remember you in my prayers."

"Yes, your prayers will be appreciated, but please don't worry about me Mrs. Galloway. I'll make out all right. I've been up against hard odds before. I'll figure out a way to rescue Hannah and her family."

Mrs. Galloway looked across the table at LaBerge and her face was now filled with a broad smile as she said, "I have an idea that you have taken a liking to this young lady and perhaps desire that she become your wife. That is most understandable and if I were in a position to do so I would not hesitate to encourage the young lady to take you as her husband. I seriously doubt if she could do better."

A broad smile came to LaBerge's face as he gazed across the table at Mrs. Galloway. "Yes, I am taken with the young lady and do intend to ask for her hand in marriage."

"If she is a wise young lady, she will accept your marriage proposal." Mrs. Galloway paused as her face took on a more serious note. "I do not like to impose upon others but considering my difficult circumstances, I will reluctantly accept your offer of further assistance. James and I shall remain here at the inn until you return. I have funds to pay for the inn and to compensate the doctor. Hopefully, the additional time will allow for a full recovery by James before we resume our journey."

They finished their meal and returned to the room where the doctor was treating James. They remained silent, standing along the wall of the small room. as the doctor and his attendant continued to hover over James. Several minutes passed, and then the doctor went to a basin of water and washed his hands. As he dried his hands he turned to Mrs. Galloway, his face reflecting his somber mood as he said, "I've removed the ball and cleansed and dressed his wound. He has been seriously injured and must not be moved for a good spell. I'll look in on him twice a day as long as is needed."

The next morning LaBerge and Mrs. Galloway went to the sheriff's office, where they met the circuit judge and gave their testimony as to the actions and conduct of the two men, Shad and Retford. who had attempted to rob Mrs. Galloway and had shot James.

The judge did not delay his ruling and before the day was gone had sentenced the men to three years of hard labor.

With that matter behind them LaBerge turned to Mrs. Galloway. "I'll be leaving to go to the rescue of the girl and her family first thing in the morning, but before I go, I'm going to check and make sure that Calvert has left the settlement. We haven't seen the man, but I want to make sure he has left. He immediately inquired of the innkeeper and was told that the man had not left and, in fact, was at this moment drinking ale in the tavern bar.

LaBerge turned from the tavern keeper and went immediately to the bar. He stopped just inside the dimly let room and let his eyes roam across occupants that were seated at the scattered tables. Within moments he saw Calvert, seated at a table as he nursed a tankard of ale. Without hesitation LaBerge strode across the room. When he halted at the edge of the table the portly man looked up at him with mingled surprise and anger spread across his face as he demanded, "What do you want?"

Laberge maintained a calm voice as he said, "I told you yesterday to leave this settlement and I'm surprised to see that you are still here! Why? What's holding you up?"

Calvert jumped to his feet like a scared jack rabbit. His movements were so clumsy that his bottle of ale went tumbling across the table and onto the sawdust covering the floor. His fat face was flushed and red as he shouted, "I'm not leaving the settlement! I'll not be pushed around by you or anyone else. And besides, I'm not through with that woman, Galloway." Calvert looked at LaBerge through bloodshot eyes as he shouted. "I'll see to it that Mrs. Galloway signs those deeds if I have to force the pen to her hand at gunpoint."

Calvert paused for a moment as he looked at Laberge with a broad sneer across his face. "I see you don't have your dog here to protect you. Ha! Ha! I can handle the likes of you. I've been in a few fights before."

LaBerge had learned that attempts to reason with these types of men was hopeless. The only thing they understood was brute force.

His response to this outburst was swift and instantaneous, as he drove his left fist hard into the man's middle, knocking the breath from him. He immediately followed this blow with a hard thrust to the fat man's face and chin. The force of this blow sent Calvert sprawling back across the floor, knocking over two chairs and spilling several bottles of ale onto the floor as men scrambled to escape the cascading man. LaBerge stepped forward and jerked the panting man back onto his feet as he said, Get your things together. You're leaving the settlement; *now!*"

Thirty minutes later LaBerge escorted Calvert from the settlement and rode with him for several miles east. When LaBerge drew his horse to a halt, he looked at Calvert as he said, "Calvert, you keep on going, and don't return to harass Mrs. Galloway about signing those deeds. Understand this, Mr. Calvert. I'm not a man to be trifled with; I'll do what I promise. And I promise you that I'll come looking for you if you return and take up harassing Mrs. Galloway or Mr. Patterson again. You keep that in mind as you ride on east." Calvert stared at LaBerge with hard eyes for several moments, but said nothing, and then abruptly turned his horse and rode away.

LaBerge watched the man's receding back until the trail took him into a stand of trees, and he was lost from his sight. He turned his horse and rode back toward Williamson and Mrs. Galloway. He wasn't sure that Calvert would follow his advice.

CHAPTER 12

Hannah Escapes

Hannah held her breath as she tip-toed across the small cabin toward the door. She moved on stocking feet, carrying her moccasins and a small bag in her hand. She paused at the door and looked back across the dark room. She could barely see her parents as they lay sleeping on their cots. Would she be able to escape and find help for her and her parents? Would she ever see them again? These troubling thoughts raced through her mind as she stared into the dark gloom of the silent room. She carefully lifted the door latch and then slowly pulled it open. As the door began to move, she prayed that it wouldn't squeak and awaken her parents, especially her father. Her father had said, shortly after they had arrived at the Roost, that he would help her escape, but despite this assurance she was reluctant to actually ask for his assistance. She harbored doubts if he would, in fact, let her go alone out into the wilderness to find help, especially after the assault Kilkenny had made upon her. She hadn't told either of her parents of her plans to attempt to escape tonight, feeling that the less they knew the better. When her absence was discovered, Kilkenny would question her parents. It would be better if they could honestly say that they knew nothing of her escape. She would leave tonight, and her mother and father would discover her absence when daylight came.

To her relief the door opened with hardly a sound, and she quickly stepped from the log cabin and slowly pulled the door closed. A dark, moonless night shrouded the Roost as she slipped on her moccasins. She moved along the front of the log structure for several stcps and then stood against the building, hoping that she was invisible against the dark structure. Her eyes roamed over the rocky grounds of the enclave, which had been their prison for over a week, and she carefully surveyed the several cabins where she hoped their captors were all sleeping. She continued her vigil for several minutes as she attempted to discern any movement about the cabins or the grounds. During the day, a guard was always posted on a high promontory overlooking the entrance to the Roost, but she had observed that he usually left his post shortly after nightfall.

As near as she had been able to discern, no man had ever been posted to directly guard the cabin where she and her parents were being held. Apparently, Kilkenny felt that the location of the Roost was so remote and difficult to reach, that neither she, nor her parents would attempt an escape through the wild mountain wilderness.

The dark gloom of the night enveloped the cabins and the grounds of the Roost, holding them tight in its dismal grasp. An oppressive silence engulfed the Roost and it seemed to Hannah that even the crickets had ceased their chirping. There was no moon and the stars seemed to have dimmed their light for fear of offending the god of darkness. As her eyes swept over the small compound for a second time, she almost expected to see a ghost moving silently across the enclave, but no aberration appeared, and she was relieved that no lights shown from the windows of the cabins. She continued to watch the cabins for any movement or light, and she jumped when she saw a movement at the edge of one of the cabins but was relieved to see that it was only a red fox stalking the grounds for a discarded bit of food.

She shifted her eyes across the enclave to the stand of trees that bordered the far edge of the compound. The grove of trees stood silent and dark against the night sky. As she stared at the dark mass of trees a sudden light breeze swept across the compound, kicking up tufts of dust and pushing a small tumbleweed across the grounds. The gust of wind passed and once again a hushed silence fell across the Roost.

shifted her attention back to the grove of trees. The moment of her greatest vulnerability had now come. She must cross the open ground between the cabin and the trees. Once she was safely in the trees, it was unlikely she would be detected.

She watched the grounds and the cabins for another few minutes and then she reached into the fold of her skirt and pulled out her knife. She wasn't sure just what she would do if accosted, as she crossed to the safety of the trees, but the knife in her hand gave her a measure of courage. She sucked in her breath and began to walk in long, careful strides towards the stand of trees. She could feel her heart pounding and she felt very vulnerable as she made her way across the open enclave toward the sanctuary of the trees. The distance was only a few hundred yards, but it seemed like miles to her. Her eyes continued to dart about the grounds as she walked, half expecting to see a man jump from the darkness and grab her. After what seemed to be an eternity she slipped into the refuge of the trees and then stopped and looked back across to the cabin where her parents lay sleeping. After a moment she shifted her gaze to each of the other cabins. They all remained dark and only the lonely moan of the night wind broke the heavy silence of the night.

She returned the knife to the sheath and her breathing became easier as she moved through the trees toward the trail that led down the mountain. The oxen had pulled the wagon up this rough, steep trail during daylight, and she was sure it would be much more difficult and dangerous to traverse during the heavy darkness of the night, but she had no choice, she had to go down the mountain to escape these evil men. As she cautiously began making her way along the rough trail and moved slowly down the mountain, putting distance between her and the Roost, hope rose in her heart. She was free! Free at last to find help.

She kept her eyes glued to the dim trail that lay before her as she attempted to discern the ruts, rocks, and obstructions that she knew cluttered the trail. Hope continued to fill her heart and then suddenly her toe caught on a root that protruded just above the ground, sending her sprawling forward onto the rough ground. She stifled a cry, as pain shot through her hands and knees from the shock of the hard fall. She struggled back to her feet, stood for a moment as she regained her breath, and to let the pain subside, and then she trudged on down the mountainside. Bruised hands and knees were a small price to pay for one's freedom, and with renewed determination she pushed on in her quest for help.

She tried to walk more carefully to avoid falling but despite her caution she fell several times as her feet caught on unseen rocks, debris, and roots that littered the dark and treacherous trail. In the darkness she was unable to see the cuts and bruises on her knees, arms, and hands, but she could feel the stinging pain. Her ankle-length skirt was probably torn and dirty, but that caused her no concern, as a torn and dirty dress was a small price to pay for her and her parents' freedom, if such could be obtained.

About two hours after starting down the trail she came upon a small stream. She immediately slumped down on a log to rest. As her breathing became easier, she went to the stream and bathed her hands and face in the cool water and then she pulled up her skirt and washed the bruises on her knees and legs. She then cupped her hands and dipped water up to quench her thirst. When her thirst was satisfied, she removed her long knife from the sheath in the fold of her dress. The bottom of her dress fell almost to the ground and impeded her progress. She would throw modesty to the winds and cut off the bottom three inches of the skirt. It took her about ten minutes to cut away a narrow, three-inch strip from the bottom of her skirt. When this was done, she returned the knife to the sheath and then folded up the strip of cloth and tucked it into the small bag she was carrying which held a few personal items. Due to her circumstances, she would not discard the strip of cloth as it might be useful to her and if she discarded it someone from the Roost might find it, giving them a hint concerning her escape.

She stood to her feet and continued her slow flight down the mountain. She moved along the trail they had come up in the wagon, but she felt that she should seek shelter away from the trail when daylight approached. She hoped to put several miles between her and the Roost before seeking a place where she could rest while waiting for daylight to return.

Her destination tomorrow was a small cabin she had seen when they were being taken to the Roost. As Kilkenny had urged the oxen up along the trail that bordered Wolf Creek, she had seen a cabin, about a mile below the large beaver dam and the turnoff. It was a remote and wild area and she had not seen any dwellings for many miles until she had noticed the small cabin, tucked into a stand of trees on the far side of Wolf Creek. Was the cabin occupied or abandoned? If occupied, would the occupants be friendly and willing to help her, or would she have only exchanged one problem for another? It was a roll of the dice; a gamble she was willing to take.

It seemed she had been making her way down this trail for many hours and her legs and arms ached from the repeated falls. She glanced up at the dark sky, but the moonless night told her little of the time, nevertheless she was sure that morning was but a short while away. Finding a relatively level place she left the trail and began making her way through the dark and rocky hillsides in what she hoped was the general direction of her destination.

A half hour later she came to a rocky overhang that afforded a small place of concealment and shelter. She slumped down onto the leaves that littered the ground under the overhang and gave a sigh of relief to be off her feet. Every bone and muscle in her body seemed to be bursting with pain. Even with the shortened dress she had fallen several times, and her knees, elbows and hands were cut and bleeding. She sat in the silence of the darkness as she rubbed her ankles, and she was about to smooth out a place to lie down when she heard the faint sound of dripping water. It was very dark under the overhang, and she could see very little. Carefully she moved toward the sound of the dripping water. She gave a small cry of joy when her outstretched hands suddenly felt cold water. She quickly discerned that it was a tiny stream of water, only a few inches wide, that was fed by the steady drip of water from the overhang above. She wet her hands in the little stream and once again bathed her cut and bruised ankles, knees, and arms. She then cupped her hand, as she held it in the little stream and let it fill with water, and then lapped up the small amount of water from her hand. She did this several times before her thirst was finally quenched. She crawled back a few feet from the water and taking her bag as a pillow she lay down. Within a few minutes the steady drip of the water had lulled her tired body into a deep sleep.

Sunlight was filtering through the trees when she awoke. She sat up and looked about, first at the rock wall that rose above her, and then at the little stream that trickled away from the wall. The sight of the water made her realize that she was thirsty and hungry, and she cupped her hands and caught water that she lapped up, quenching her thirst.

She turned her gaze from the trickle of water to look down at the steep mountainside of rocks, trees, and brush that lay below her. She was glad that she had stopped at the overhang and not attempted to go down this treacherous slope during the night.

The pain from the scrapes and bruises on her arms and legs made her look away from the mountainside and direct her attention to her arms and ankles. Once again, she went to the trickle of water and bathed the bloody cuts and scrapes on her ankles, legs, and arms. The cool water seemed to take some of the pain away.

She opened the bag and took out the remnants of a sandwich she had secreted away. She had two, half sandwiches to tide her through until she could obtain food. She quickly ate the sandwich and then struggled to her feet. At first, she was unsure if she could even walk, as the pain in her feet, ankles and legs was so intense. But she had no alternative but to travel on down the mountain. Biting her lip in pain she stepped away from the trickle of water, and the shelter of the overhang, and began to make her way down the steep mountainside.

Each step sent a sharp pain shooting up her legs as she carefully made her way down the treacherous slope, clinging to boulders and small trees for support. She was unsure how much further it was until she came to Wolf Creek. The pain in her legs seemed to travel like lightning up through her body. She hoped she would reach the cabin before her legs gave out. She had descended along the steep slope for nearly a half hour when suddenly her foot caught on a root, and she pitched forward.

Desperately she attempted to grab the branch of a small tree in an attempt to arrest her fall, but the branch slipped through her fingers as she tumbled forward. Her scream cut through the forest as she fell, head over heels down the steep slope, and then her head slammed into a large boulder. The blow knocked her unconscious and she knew nothing as her body rolled on down the slope until coming to rest against the base of a large tree.

A squirrel, which had been scavenging for acorns, scurried up a tree when he heard the girl scream. He looked down on the still figure as he chattered his displeasure at this intrusion into his domain. He continued to chatter for a few minutes and then he made his way back down the tree and resumed his search for acorns. The scream of the girl had echoed across the mountainside but had now faded away, as a heavy silence reclaimed the forest.

O. L. Brown

CHAPTER 13

The Hermit

T he mountain man, trapper, hunter, and hermit, Jake Herat, had left his cabin, which was tucked into the stand of trees a short distance above Wolf Creek and had walked to the stream to fill his wooden bucket with water when the scream of a woman shattered the peace and calm of the morning.

He dropped the bucket, stood to his feet, and cocked his ear toward the sound, as he looked across the stream and up at the rocky mountain side that rose steeply away from Wolf Creek. The cry did not come again, and the only sound was the low moan of the morning breeze as it blew through the trees, and the cawing of a crow as it flew along the creek.

Herat hadn't seen a woman in over six months, but what he had just heard was definitely the cry of a woman who was in distress. It could be an Indian woman, but he doubted it. There were Iroquois and Shawnee Indians in the area. Mostly hunting parties out from their main camps some thirty miles south. He doubted if an Indian hunting party would come down that steep and rocky mountainside. They would use the well-worn trails they had used for centuries. And besides, Indian women rarely went out with hunting parties.

He filled his bucket with water and returned to his cabin. He set the bucket on a bench in the corner of the cabin, and taking a gourd dipper, he took a long drink of the cool water. The scream

111

continued to echo through his head and trouble him as he began to tidy up the cabin.

As was his nature, he quickly made a decision to go and investigate the scream. If he didn't, the cry of the woman would haunt him for days. He quickly sat down at the table and primed his long rifle and then slung the powder horn over his shoulder and strapped the shot pouch to his waist. He grabbed up his coonskin cap, from where it hung on a peg near the door, jammed it down on his head, and left the cabin. He strode in long strides to the creek and crossed the small stream on the large stones he had laid across the stream. When he had crossed the creek and the rough trail that ran along side of the creek he paused for a moment as he looked up at the steep mountain side. It was going to be a hard climb and he was unsure what he would find. Perhaps he would find the woman who had screamed, and then he might find nothing. If she were in trouble, why hadn't she called out a second time? Perhaps she was lying unconscious, or dead, and hidden by trees, brushes, or rocks. It would be like looking for a needle in a haystack. He grunted to himself as he ran his hand through his heavy whiskers. No matter, he'd give it a try, perhaps he could pick up a footprint that would lead him to her. The mountainside was steep and treacherous, but he'd tackled worse on many occasions. He began to climb in long easy strides that barely caused him to breath hard. After ten minutes of climbing his keen eye spotted the print of a moccasin in some gravel. The print was small and definitely had been made by a young woman.

Herat was a hermit who had lived in these wild mountains for several years and he could track a bear or cougar through grass or over rocks. Now that he had found one track, he was confident he'd find more. He'd find the woman now! He carefully surveyed the area and soon found another smudged track a short distance down the mountain. A few minutes passed and then he found another track. And then he saw her. She was slumped up against a tree at the bottom of a steep and treacherous slope that was strewn with rocks and debris. He watched her for a moment, and he could see that there was a bloody wound on her head, and she was crying.

Herat carefully made his way along the treacherous slope toward the woman. Her head was slumped forward into her hands, and she didn't see him until he was only a few feet from her. When she looked up and saw him her eyes were suddenly filled with fear at the sight of this bearded man, and she gave a startled cry as she attempted to jump to her feet. And then her cry turned to a scream of pain as her left leg gave way, and she fell back against the tree.

"It's alright ma'am," he called out. "I won't harm you." Herat stepped forward to her side as he said, "It looks as if you've taken a nasty fall. Yer heads all banged up and I can see that yer legs cut bad."

She quickly jerked her skirt down over her exposed leg. Men shouldn't see a woman's exposed leg; to do so was scandalous. She looked up at him with a mixture of embracement and hope, as she said, "Yes, I fell down the mountain. I've banged up my head and my left ankle hurts like the devil." She looked up at him with what he thought was a whipped dog look as she began to sob. "Mister. I . . . I hurt all over. Will you help me?"

Herat knelt at her side as he said, "Yes, ma'am, I'll help you. I live across the creek in a cabin, and I heard you scream, so I came lookin' for you."

She wiped the tears from her face with the back of her hand as she said, "Thank you. I could sure use some help. It seems I've made a mess of things!"

Herat hesitated for a moment as he fell silent, staring at her. He was a mountain man who he had little experience in dealing with woman or young girls.

Finally, he stammered, "If you will give me your hand, I'll help you up. Do you think you can walk?"

"I don't know," she said. "I hope so."

Herat stood to his feet and then reached out his hand to hers. She grasped his hand, and he pulled her up from the ground. This was about as intimate a contact as he'd ever had with a woman. She didn't weigh much and pulling her upright presented no challenge to him. She stood with all of her weight on her right foot for a moment and then placed some weight on her left foot. Instantly, she cried out in pain, and he had to grab her around the waist to keep her from falling. "I'm sorry ma'am," he exclaimed. 'I didn't mean to grab you so close, but I was afraid you would fall."

Hannah smiled for the first time since he had found her, as she said, "That's okay mister, I understand. You were just trying to help." She looked up at him as she smiled again. "With this bum ankle you're gonna need to keep a tight hold on me around the waist and I'll need to lean right hard on you to get down off this mountain."

She looked up at him and he thought he detected a twinkle in her eyes as she said, "Now, let's get down off this mountain and go to your cabin. That's where I was a headin' when I tumbled down the mountain side."

This last statement left the hermit speechless.

CHAPTER 14

The Confrontation

The violent force of being slammed against the side of the cabin knocked Jedidiah Cody's breath from him and it was with difficulty that he managed to keep from slumping to the ground as he tried to fill his lungs with air. Kilkenny made sure he didn't fall to the ground as he grabbed the collar of his shirt and pulled him so close that his face was only a few inches away, as he shouted, "When did she leave? Where did she go?"

Kilkenny shoved Cody back against the cabin with a hard thrust and then stepped away, his face filled with frustration and rage as he shouted. "You tell me, or I'll whip ya within an inch of yer life! Do you hear me?"

Cody said nothing as he struggled to get his breath. Even in his discomfort he had to stifle a grin of satisfaction. He was secretly very proud of his daughter for her ingenuity and courage in escaping from this enclave, which was their prison, but at the same time he was equally concerned for her safety. She had escaped sometime during the night and would have been making her way down the rough mountain in heavy darkness. Any number of tragedies could have befallen her, from wild animals, to falling down a steep slope or over a cliff to her death. In addition, she was unfamiliar with this wild wilderness, and where would she go? Who would she find that would be willing to come to her, and her family's aid? Someone might take her in and help her, but it was very unlikely she would find anyone who would be willing, and able, to come to the Roost and attempt to rescue her parents. An image of the tall stranger flashed through Cody's mind. If Hannah could somehow find Jean LaBerge, Cody was sure that he would come to rescue them. But how would she find him? Cody didn't know where this confrontation with Kilkenny was going to lead, and it could easily lead to the beating that he had just promised. He'd take the beating. Kilkenny wouldn't kill him because he needed him. Keeping Kilkenny believing that money was coming from the east was about the only card that he held in this crazy game that was being played out here at the Roost. Kilkenny needed him until he had the money.

Kilkenny had forced him to send a letter to the eastern bank, but of course, the letter wouldn't bring any money, for the simple fact that there was no money in the eastern bank. It remained hidden in the floor of the wagon. When Kilkenny eventually learned that there was no money in the eastern bank he would be further enraged, but in the meantime, it was also buying them time. Time for Hannah to find someone who would come to their rescue from this den of thieves.

In fact, Cody felt that Hannah's escape had given him an edge he hadn't enjoyed before. He was breathing better now as he took a confident step forward, away from the cabin toward Kilkenny, and his voice was filled with a newfound conviction as he said, "You thought we were pushovers; just a storekeeper and two helpless women. And now that my daughter has escaped you've been dealt a new hand of cards, and you don't like what you're holding and are now unsure how things may turnout for you!"

He took another step toward Kilkenny and then stopped. He glanced quickly to the doorway of the cabin where his wife stood, with frightened eyes. "It's okay Cathedra," he said, "Everything will be alright."

His wife looked at him for a moment and then she turned to Kilkenny with eyes that were filled with pain and fear but also with a newfound determination. She was deathly afraid for her daughter, but also secretly proud of what she had done. She would support her

116

family and she tried to keep any fear from her voice as she stepped from the doorway. "My husband is right," she exclaimed. Everything has changed for you now that our daughter has escaped. I'm confident that she will return with someone who will put an end to your evil scheming." She pointed her finger at Kilkenny, and her voice was filled with a new-found strength as she exclaimed. "You are the one who needs to be afraid. You will lose sleep of nights now; wondering when they will come for you." She thought of the tall stranger as she raised her voice. "When that tall man comes here to rescue us, he'll kill you Kilkenny, and I'll be happy to see you dead."

She took a quick step back as she covered her mouth. She had said too much, especially that part about being happy to see Kilkenny dead. But in her heart, she knew that she would be pleased to see this evil man, who had kidnapped her and her family, and who had attempted to assault her daughter, dead.

Kilkenny glared at Mrs. Cody for a long moment and then he shouted, "You get back into the cabin and keep your mouth shut if you know what's good for you."

The escape of her daughter had emboldened the normally mild-mannered Cathedra Cody and she had suddenly become a brave woman as she replied. "No, I'll not go inside. I'm going to stay out here and support my husband. You have no reason to hit him and abuse him. He 'didn't know our daughter was leaving last night. She never told us that she was planning to escape last night."

Cody spoke now in a firm and confident voice as he said, "Our daughter is a lot smarter than you thought! She escaped last night, and you don't know where she has gone and who will come back with her to rescue us." A cross between a smile and a sneer came to Cody's face as he continued, "Why, like my wife said, she'll most likely return with that tall stranger that we met on the flatboat. I got to know him well during our travels down the Ohio River and I can tell you that he's a brave and determined man. You'll have your hands full if he comes here to rescue us!"

Cody snickered as he continued. "You sent two of your men to rob him, perhaps to even kill him, but over a week has passed and they haven't returned." He paused as he looked at Kilkenny, and his voice was filled with sarcasm as he said, "I wonder what has happened to your two men? Why haven't they returned?"

Kilkenny's face was now flushed with rage as he shouted, "You shut yer mouth old man, or I'll smash yer face in! That would shut ya up for a while."

Taggert, who was standing a few feet away, spoke. "Take it easy boss. I doubt if there's much to worry about. This is rough country. The girl left here sometime during the night. There was no moon last night and she'd find walking down the mountain trail, and away from here, mighty hard. He lowered his voice as he continued, "My guess is she's probably laying at the bottom of a ravine with a broken neck! That's most likely what has happened to her."

A shudder went through Cody's heart as he heard Taggert. He was deathly afraid that what Taggert had just said could be true, but he wouldn't let these men know of his concerns for his daughter's wellbeing. "You don't know my daughter" he said. "She can see in the dark like a cat. She'll make it down the mountain and she'll find help. And when she returns, I wouldn't want to be in your shoes!"

Kilkenny was unable to contain his rage as he rushed forward and jabbed Cody across the face with a hard swing of his fist. The force of the blow sent Cody sprawling back against the side of the cabin. Slowly Cody pulled himself up to a sitting position as he wiped the blood from his face with the sleeve of his shirt. He looked up at Kilkenny with eyes that were steady and sure as he said, "There will come a day of reckoning for you Kilkenny. And when it comes, I wouldn't want to be in your boots."

Cathedra Cody had quickly stepped to the side of her husband. She glared at Kilkenny as she said, "You're an awful and despicable man! What my husband said is quite true. There *will* be a day of reckoning for you and may the good Lord have mercy on you when it comes!"

118

Kilkenny backed away under her steady gaze and then he turned to Taggert as he said, "I want you and Keaton to get out onto the trail and see if you can pick up the girls tracks. If you can, follow them and see if you can determine if she made it out." He snickered as he glanced at Cody. "It's more likely they will find her body at the bottom of a cliff or ravine. I doubt she made it out."

"Sure," said Keaton. "We'll take a look and see what we can find."

As Kilkenny turned from Taggert, he saw Belle Turk striding toward him. Kilkenny winced as he watched Turk approach. More trouble was on the way.

Turk was twenty paces away when he began bellowing in a loud voice. "Kilkenny, what's this I hear about that young girl escaping last night?"

Kilkenny tried to put the best possible face on a bad situation as he replied, "It's nothing much. She's just a young girl, who's most likely lost, or lying dead at the bottom of a ravine with her neck busted. It's nothin' ta worry yourself about."

Turk halted two paces away as he glared at Kilkenny, his arms waving in the air and his voice carrying across the enclave as he exclaimed, "Yeah, that's cheap enough for ya to say, but she's gone and ya don't know if she made it out or not!" He stopped waving his arms and thrust out his hand at Kilkenny as he pointed at him with a fat finger. "If she made it back down ta Wolf Creek, she'll most likely run into somebody, and began blabbering on about this place. Hell, she may even lead someone back up here to rescue her parents." He paused for a moment, his face filled with anger and frustration. "I told ya it was a mistake for ya ta bring those people up here and I told ya when ya came to leave the next morning, but ya are still here. And now see what has happened! Ya have let the girl escape. I want . . ."

Kilkenny interrupted the tirade as he said, "I've instructed my two men, Taggart and Keaton to get out immediately and see if they can pick up her trail, and if they can, to follow her tracks and see where they lead, but I doubt she even made it out. They'll likely find her body before noon."

Turk glared at Kilkenny for a long moment, his face flushed with anger, his voice loud and harsh. "You find that girl, dead or alive! In the meantime, I'm gonna send a couple of my men down to the trailhead at the beaver dam to guard the trail leading up here to the Roost."

Belle Turk stepped directly in front of Kilkenny, stopped and glared at him for a long moment, his face filled with anger. "You see if you can find that girl today and then I want the lot of ya out of here! I've had it with ya!" He glared at Kilkenny for a long moment and then turned and stalked toward his cabin.

Kilkenny slowly let out his breath in relief as he watched Belle Turk walk away. He turned to Taggert and Keaton. "You heard what I said to Turk. See if you can pick up the girls tracks and follow them. Perhaps you can find her; dead or alive."

CHAPTER 15

Hannah's Plea

Jake Herat stared across the small cabin at the girl, his whiskered face filled with frustration. *Women! They could drive a man nuts. They were always so sure they were right and knew just what was best for someone else to do.* She was the first encounter he'd had with a woman in many months, and he hoped it would be the last for many years. Escaping the clutches of demanding and designing women had been one of the reasons he'd left the farms and towns of the east and journeyed to the wilderness to live alone in a cabin. And now he was stuck with this demanding woman he had rescued a few days ago and he could see that she was going to be hard to chuck. She was a small wildcat; a ball of spitfire and determination, who paid little attention to his protests against her ideas and pleas. He had begun to question why he had gone up the mountain to rescue her. Bringing her here to his cabin had disrupted the peace, quiet, and daily routine of his life.

There she was, sitting on the edge of *his* bed, looking at him with that determined look on her face he had learned to expect whenever she wanted something. She had taken over his bunk as well as a large chunk of his life. He'd been pushed outside to sleep under an oak tree. Luckily, it hadn't rained. He was thankful for a few small favors the Lord had sent his way. A makeshift bandage, he had made from one of his bandannas, was wrapped around the bruise on the side of her head. It was a poor and goofy looking bandage which he had contrived, but to his surprise she hadn't complained. However, the blow to her head hadn't seemed to have knocked any sense into her. This was evident by what she was saying now, for what seemed like the tenth time. "Mr. Herat, we must leave tomorrow and go and rescue my parents. I've been here several days now, and we must not delay any longer!"

"Miss Cody, "he sputtered, exasperation written across his face. "I don't seem to be making myself clear to you. I'm not gonna go up there and take on Belle Turk and that band of outlaws and desperadoes singlehanded. That knock on yer head must have addled yer brain some, if ya think I'm that dumb."

"But I told you Mr. Herat, I'll go with you and help you. I can travel now. I'm feeling much better, and we must not delay for another day." She paused as she looked at him from where she was seated on his bed, and he thought he could detect both fear and hope written across her face as she said, "With your help, Mr. Herat, I believe we can outwit Turk, Kilkenny, and the other men and take my parents away during the night. I think we can avoid an actual confrontation with them and will have left before they are aware that we have been there."

Herat threw up his hands in exasperation as he exclaimed, "Girl, taking you along would most likely make things worse as I would be concerned for your safety as well as my own. It's likely we'd both be taken prisoner or even killed. It's nuts to go up there!" He paused as he paced across the floor of the cabin and then he turned to her with a hopeful look on his face. "Tell ya what I'll do! I'll take ya to the sheriff in Williamson and see if he's willin' ta help ya rescue yer Ma and Pa. I . . . I'll do that for ya!" He managed a broader smile through his whiskers as he said, "We'll leave first thing in the morning."

She had left his cot and was on her feet now and had moved a step toward him. Her face carried one of those know-it-alls looks that he'd seen on the face of women before, as she said, "No, we will *not* waste time going to the sheriff in Williamson. It's very simple Mr. Herat; I know my way around the Roost, and we'll slip in there while it's dark tomorrow night and rescue my parents and get Pa's money and then leave while it's still dark. We can do it in the dark. I got out of there at night, and we can get in at night. We'll rescue my parents tomorrow!" Herat stood near the door of his cabin, staring at the girl, disbelief written across his face. As was usual with women, they glossed over the most important and difficult matters and tried to make everything appear to be so simple and easy, but he knew better. His voice was filled with frustration as he said, "Even if we get in undetected, how are we all going to leave the place? Are we just going to round up the oxen, hitch them to the wagon, and all ride out in that contraption?" He snickered, "Not likely!"

She was silent for a moment, which he took as a hopeful sign, and then she said, "I . . . I'm not sure, but we'll think of something, but we must go to the Roost and try and rescue my parents! And we must do it tomorrow!"

She stopped speaking and looked at him, her eyes had grown soft and were now filled with pleading as she said in a soft voice. "Please, Mr. Herat. Please help me rescue my parents. Surely, we can find a way to rescue my Ma and Pa!" She paused for a moment, and then continued, her voice filled with melancholy. "If you won't help me, I guess I'll just have to take one of your pistols and go back there by myself. I suppose you would at least let me use one of your pistols?"

Herat left the door, walked to the table, and took a chair. He knew that she was now playing to his weakness, as she pleaded for his help and the use of one of his weapons. He sat in silence for a long minute, thinking and pondering. It galled him but he realized that he couldn't refuse her request for help. He looked across the little room at her as he said, "Here's what we can do. I've got some extra horses. We'll each ride a horse and lead an extra horse behind us. That way your parents will each have a horse to ride out on. In addition, we can't just go riding up the trail into the hideout, even in the dark, as they'll most likely have a lookout posted at the overlook just below the camp, but I know of an old Indian Trail that we can take that will get us there, most likely undetected." He paused for a moment and then he continued. "We'll leave our horses tethered some distance from the hideout and then go on in afoot. I think it might work. We won't be able to take out anything except yer Pa's money, but I guess that's a small enough price to be paid for being rescued."

She jumped to her feet as she said, "Oh, you're a wonderful man, Mr. Herat! I knew you would help me!

CHAPTER 16

The Roost

The late afternoon sun cast dancing shadows through the trees as Jean LaBerge paused to catch his breath. Even for a young man in his prime the steep climb up the east side of Flag Knob Mountain had been difficult and strenuous and had left him breathing hard.

The trapper, Sykes, had told him that the rough trail leading up the steep mountain to the Roost was located a short distance past the large beaver dam on Wolf Creek. After leaving Mrs. Galloway he had made his way to Wolf Creek and had then cautiously worked his way up along the creek. He thought it likely that there would be at least one guard posted at the trail head that led to the Roost and he intended to avoid alerting the guard or guards to his presence.

He had detected the presence of the beaver dam before he reached it by observing the subtle change in the water flow of the creek. He'd left his horse in a grove of trees, and keeping to the cover of trees and rocks, had proceeded on foot until he spotted the beaver dam and the turnoff that Sykes had mentioned. He hadn't been surprised to see a man lounging near the entrance to the turnoff, a long rifle in his hands. From heavy cover he'd studied the man and the area for several minutes. He could probably overpower the man and then make his way directly up the trail to the Roost, but mindful of the advice of the trapper he elected to make the climb to the precipice overlooking the Roost and come in from above.

He had returned to his horse and ridden back down along the creek for about a mile. When he came to a small rivulet of a stream that came bubbling down the mountainside he turned and rode into the forest along the stream until he came to a small meadow. He had slipped his horse's bridle to allow him to graze and had patted him on the shoulder as he said, "Stay here boy. There's grass and water for you. I may be gone for several hours, perhaps even a day, but I'll return." He turned to his dog. "Come on Shag. Let's you and I climb this mountain together." Shag had vigorously waged his tail and scrambled along behind him as he began his assent up the steep face of the mountain.

He'd now made his way to a spot that he believed would allow him to look down onto the Roost. He carefully made his way forward and as he neared the edge of the precipice he went down to his knees and crawled forward and then eased in behind a bush that would give him cover from anyone who was watching from below. He then slipped down onto his belly and eased around the edge of the bush. He pulled himself forward until he could look down onto the camp that lay scattered below him. With discerning eyes, which missed little, and a keen attention to detail, he carefully surveyed the scene spread out below him. He could see five rough log cabins, scattered haphazardly about the enclave. A wagon, which he thought was the Cody wagon, was parked near the front on one of the cabins.

At the far-right edge of the grounds a large, three-sided pole structure, with a brush roof, had been constructed, to apparently serve as an enclosure for the men's horses during inclement weather. Beyond the pole enclosure he could see a large grassy meadow where several horses and mules, a few cows, and two oxen grazed. The presence of the oxen and the wagon strongly suggested that he had found the Roost, where Hannah and her parents were being held.

He observed this scene for several minutes and then a movement caught his eye as a tall, muscular man walked from the cabin that stood near the center of the hideaway. The man proceeded on across the enclave toward one of the cabins. As he neared the cabin a man stepped out and waited for him, his hands resting on his hips.

LaBerge continued to watch the two men as they came together and began to converse with gesturing and what appeared to be loud talk, although he could not hear their voices. From time to time the large man appeared very agitated as he waved his hands and arms, and once LaBerge caught the faint sound of the big man's voice as he shouted at the other man. Perhaps this tall, heavy man was the captain or leader of the men who frequented this hideout. Sykes had told him that the leader of the gang that frequented the hideout was a man whose name was Belle Turk. "I'm not acquainted with him," he said, "I saw him once at a tavern in Williamson. He's tall and heavy and I understand he's a hard man, although I know nothing more about him,"

LaBerge couldn't be sure, due to the distance, but the smaller of the two men, appeared to be the man who had been the leader of the five men who had rode into the settlers camp the night after they had left the flatboat. If he remembered correctly, the man's name was Kilkenny.

LaBerge momentarily shifted his gaze from the two men and glanced behind him to check on his dog. He gave a grunt of satisfaction. Shag had found refuge under a small tree where he had curled up and fallen asleep.

He turned his attention back to the scene that lay below him and continued to watch the two men. As he observed their animated exchange, he formed the opinion that there was considerable animosity between the men. Perhaps those bad feelings could be used to his advantage.

His attention was suddenly diverted away from the men as a movement near the cabin where the wagon was parked caught his attention. He watched as Hannah's mother stepped from the cabin and walked to the corner of the structure, where she stood in the shadows watching the two men as they conversed. He gave a grunt of satisfaction. He now knew for sure which cabin held the Cody family. He continued to watch Mrs. Cody and hoped that he would catch a glimpse of Hannah, but he was disappointed as she made no appearance.

The climb up the mountain to this overlook had been hard, dangerous, and slow. He'd been determined to avoid detection and hadn't encountered any sentries guarding the precipice above the camp. Now that he was here at the overlook he understood why. It was a very difficult climb, up steep, rocky slopes, and the occupants of the camp probably felt that this difficulty made it extremely unlikely that they would be attacked from above. The advice Sykes had given him, to come in from above, had been good counsel.

His attention went back to the two men as they parted. The big man was shouting at the other and it was evident to LaBerge that the parting was not amicable. It was only a guess, but he surmised that the anger between the two men centered on the Cody family and their captivity by Kilkenny.

LaBerge glanced up at the sun that hung low in the western sky above the deep blue mountains. The sun would set soon, and darkness was only a few hours away. It was his intention to attempt a rescue of Hannah and her parents sometime during the night. Exactly how he was to accomplish this filled his active mind. A multitude of items needed to be considered if he hoped to be successful.

Perhaps his biggest challenge was how to get Hannah's parents down the steep and rough mountain. It would be very difficult for them to make their way swiftly down the mountain during the darkness of the night, especially if they were walking. He would need three horses: one for Hannah and one for each of her parents. He looked back toward the meadow and the grazing horses. Somehow, he would need to roundup three of these horses and get them saddled. He thought on this for a few minutes and then abandoned the idea. It would be nearly impossible to gather three horses undetected. He would need to find another way to get the Cody family down the mountain.

All these questions filled his mind as he looked down from the precipice above the camp. He'd take the challenges one at a time, moving from step to step. His first action would be to make his way undetected into the camp and to the cabin where he believed Hannah and her parents were being held.

He would then get them out of the camp and find a hiding place for them until he could return with horses and take them away. Perhaps it was a good plan, but he had also learned that things rarely went according to plan. Something always came up that altered the best laid plans. He was sure he would need to adjust and improvise as the rescue got underway.

He slipped back away from the overlook and taking the dog he spent a half hour scouting the area until he found the faint Indian trail, Sykes had spoken of that led down the edge of the precipice. This was the trail he would descend when darkness shrouded the area. It would be a difficult descent in the dark, but he would not risk detection during the daylight.

He returned to the overlook and made himself comfortable as he seated himself against a tree a short distance back from the edge of the precipice. From time to time, he slipped forward and looked down on the enclave, but there was very little activity as the deep shadows of the coming night began to fall across the Roost.

The sun slipped silently behind the far blue mountains and heavy darkness chased away the evening light. As the night deepened the stars began to make their silent appearance as a pale half-moon cast earie shadows across the Roost. LaBerge turned to his dog. "Come on boy, we've got work to do." On moccasin clad feet, Jean LaBerge began to make his way down the steep Indian trail that would take him to the Roost. His dog scrambled along behind him.

CHAPTER 17

Showdown at the Roost

T he pale half-moon cast an ethereal light across the Roost and danced across the dust motes in Belle Turk's cabin. Inside the cabin, barely four feet separated the stark figures of Belle Turk and Kilkenny as they glared at each other with hate filled eyes. Their shoulders and arms tense and bulging in anticipation of the showdown which had apparently arrived.

Turk's eyes appeared to be about to spring from their sockets, his right-hand hovered menacingly just above the handle of his long bowie knife, and his left hand gripped the back of a chair. Kilkenny's shoulders bulged against his buckskin shirt, his legs were spread apart, his arms tense, his jaw firm, and his eyes blazing in defiance. He held his Kentucky long rifle high at his side, his finger on the trigger, and the long barrel of the rifle pointed ominously at Turk's bulging middle. Except for the heavy breathing of the two men, an ominous silence gripped the cabin as the men glared at each other with anger, hate, and frustration spread across their faces. From the far edge of the Roost an owl hooted its mournful call, as if anticipating the coming outburst of violence.

Belle Turk broke the silence of the cabin as he yelled, his eyes blazing in fury, "I've had enough of ya, Kilkenny! You'll leave at first light tomorrow morning, and you'll take the Cody's with ya. I'm sick of ya and yer motley crew." His face was filled with venom as he nearly shouted, "I told ya this mornin' and then again, this afternoon, to pack up and get out, but ya have ignored me. You'll be out of here by shortly after sunup or I'll kill ya! Now be gone and get to packin.' I've had it with ya!"

Kilkenny's grip on the long rifle tightened as he raised it higher along his side. His face was filled with rage and frustration as he yelled back at Turk. "I ain't leavin' until I've got Cody's money. He wrote the bank back east and requested that the funds be forwarded to the bank in Williamson. The mail is slow, but it'll be here within a few days. I'm not leaving . . ."

"Ah yer nuts," interrupted Turk. "That man ain't got any money, and if he has it's not a gonna come to the bank in Williamson. I say yer dreamin'."

"I'm not leavin'" yelled Kilkenny. "You can't order me around and tell me when to leave here. I won't stand for it! I've as much right to be here as you! So back off and leave me be!"

"I've given ya fair warning," yelled Turk. "You'll leave or I'll kill ya."

"No, I'll not leave!" yelled Kilkenny, "If you force my hand, I'll kill you. I ain't afraid of you! You ain't as tough as you think you are."

Turk's response to this outburst was instantaneous and swift, as he yelled, "Yeah, I'll show ya how tough I am!" For a large man he moved with surprising agility as he swept up the chair with his left hand and swung it hard across the barrel of Kilkenny's long rifle, knocking it from his hand as it exploded, sending the ball into the floor of the cabin. As the rifle fired Turk jerked the bowie knife from its sheath with his right hand. He gripped the big knife in his huge fist as he advanced a step toward Kilkenny and his voice was shrill and filled with rage and determination as he yelled. "I'm gonna cut ya up some Kilkenny. You'll leave here a bloody mess, or dead!"

Kilkenny retreated a step as stark fear suddenly swept over him. He knew he was no match in a knife fight with the huge man. His defiance and courage suddenly evaporated as he turned and fled toward the door of the cabin. As he jerked desperately at the latch Turk threw the knife, which sped across the small room and slammed into the left side of Kilkenny's back. Kilkenny's scream of pain echoed across the Roost as he thrust the door open and stumbled out into the darkness of the night with Turk's knife protruding from his back.

******

The sharp gunshot and scream brought Jedidiah Cody to his feet from where he'd been sitting on the edge of the cot. He cast a quick and troubled look at his wife as he exclaimed, "There's trouble afoot, Ma! Something has happened. I'm not sure, but it sounded like the gunshot, and the scream came from the direction of Turk's cabin." He looked across the small room at his wife as he said, "A fight's been brewing between Turk and Kilkenny and perhaps it's broken out into the open. One of them may be dead or seriously wounded."

Cathedra Cody had been laying on her cot. At the sound of the shot and scream, she had quickly scrambled to her feet. "Yes, I don't believe it bodes well," she said as she stared at the door of the cabin and then turned and looked at her husband. "I think you're right about a fight brewing between those men. Turk and Kilkenny had a row in front of his cabin earlier today. I was standing in the shade of our cabin and could see them as they argued, although I don't think they noticed me as they were so engrossed in their argument. I could tell that both men were a. angry and riled up. I couldn't hear what was said, but I suspect it had something to do with us. I think Turk may have ordered Kilkenny, perhaps for the final time, to take us and leave."

"Yes, Turk has never been pleased that Kilkenny brought us here. It's been some time now, and I think he's getting antsy. Based on what little I've been able to pick up, I'm sure Turk wants the lot of us gone from here."

Cody walked to the door of the little cabin. He cautiously opened the door and stepped out into the night. He made his way to the corner of the cabin, being careful to remain in the dark shadows as he looked toward Turk's cabin. In the darkness, he could make out several figures kneeling beside a man who was lying on the ground near the front of the cabin."

Cathedra stepped to his side as she peered into the darkness. "Who is it? Can you tell who is laying on the ground?"

"No, I can't tell who it is, but it appears that he has been seriously injured."

Cathedra gripped her husband's arm as she looked up at him with fear in her eyes. "What are we going to do?" she whispered. "I'm scared Jedidiah!"

******

When the sharp report of the gunshot reverberated across the Roost and into the grove of trees Jake Herat had instinctively reached out and placed a restraining hand on Hannah Cody's arm. The gunshot was followed almost immediately by a scream and then the door to a cabin was thrust open and in the pale light from the cabin they saw a man stumble out and then fall to the ground.

They were hunkered down in the grove of trees at the edge of the enclave, waiting until all of the men had retired for the night and the lights in the cabins had all fallen dark, before attempting to make their way across the open enclave to the cabin where Hannah's parents were be being held captive.

"There's something going on," exclaimed Herat, in a voice that was barely above a whisper. "A gunshot and scream, sounds bad, but it's hard to determine what's happened, especially in the dark." He squinted into the darkness as he continued, "Several men have gathered near the man who ran from the cabin and fell to the ground. I think perhaps he's been shot."

Herat continued to hold her arm in a firm grip as he said in a low voice, "Take it easy missy. We'll just hold on here for a spell while things calm down and everyone has gone to bed. We'll make our move then."

******

Jean LaBerge had nearly completed his descent along the steep trail leading from the precipice when he was startled by the sharp gunshot as it shattered the silence of the night. He had been through a war, and he knew that the scream that followed the gunshot had come from a man who had experienced deep and sudden pain. He immediately paused on the trail and stood looking about for a long moment, listening for any further sounds that might give him a clue as to what was happening. His dog, Shag, stood at his side, making low intermittent growls. He patted the dog on the head as he said, "It's okay boy." There were no more gunshots or screams, but through the darkness he could hear the shouts and curses of men.

He resumed his descent along the steep trail until he had reached the edge of the Roost. He stood in a stand of trees, listening to the sounds of the men and looking into the darkness of the Roost, as he attempted to discern what was going on.

After a moment he left the trees and made his way closer to the cabin where the men were clustered just outside the door of a cabin and knelt behind a large boulder. Within moments he saw a man, with a lantern in his hand, emerge from a cabin and walk briskly toward where the men were clustered together. When the man sat the lantern on the ground, LaBerge could see that a man was laying on the ground and was being tended to by some of the men.

Several minutes passed as he continued to watch the cluster of men, and then two of the men lifted the downed man to his feet and helped him to move across the enclave and into a cabin.

Several men continued to loiter for several minutes near where the man had been laying, speaking in harsh tones and raised voices. He remained behind the boulder, waiting and watching and within half an hour the men parted and made their way to various cabins.

Except for the soft moan of the wind in the trees a heavy silence now lay across the Roost. A half hour later LaBerge watched a red fox as it trotted about the camp in search of a scrap of food. The

O. L. Brown

movement of the fox suggested to LaBerge that everyone was now inside a cabin.

He was anxious to be about his mission, but he would wait and watch until it was likely that everyone was in bed and hopefully asleep. Over the course of the next two hours the dim light, coming from the windows of the cabins, all went out.

LaBerge glanced up through the trees at the mist shrouded moon that hung in the western sky. From its position he judged it was well past midnight. He had not detected any guards about the camp, but he couldn't be sure. He was ready to make his way to the cabin where he believed the Cody family were being held.

He had just begun to rise up from his position behind the boulder when a movement across on the far side of the enclave caught his attention. He quickly ducked back behind the boulder and watched as two shadowy figures emerged from a stand of trees and began to make their way across the enclave. To LaBerge's discerning eyes it appeared that they were making their way toward the cabin that he believed held Jedidiah Cody and his family.

Suddenly LaBerge sucked in his breath as he gasped. *"It's the girl, Hannah! What . . . what's going on?"* He continued to watch as Hannah and a man moved swiftly toward the cabin.

As Hannah and her companion approached the cabin a man stepped suddenly out from behind the far side of the small cabin. LaBerge could clearly hear him as he called out, "Halt where you are!" The sudden appearance of the man startled LaBerge. The man had been on the far side of the cabin and hidden from his view. Were the other cabins similarly guarded?

Hannah and the man came to a halt about fifty feet from the entrance to the cabin. As the man approached them LaBerge could see a pistol in his hand, and he watched as they spoke in low tones for a few minutes and then all three went into the cabin. Within a few minutes a pale light shone from the window of the cabin.

LaBerge was up on his feet now. He wasn't sure of the exact meaning of what he had just witnessed, but he was sure it didn't bode

135

well for the Cody family. He hadn't expected to see Hannah and a strange man running across the enclave. Apparently, she had escaped and had returned with this man in an effort to rescue her parents, only to be apprehended even before they could gain access to her parent's cabin. He gritted his teeth in determination; he'd deal with this new development, one way or another.

The dog, Shag, was crouched at his side as LaBerge stepped from the boulder. He looked down at the dog as he muttered. "Come on Shag. We have our work cut out for us."

Man, and dog quickly melted into the night as they made their way along the periphery of the Roost, shielded by trees and shrubs until they were at spot where he could come up on the small cabin from the rear. He drew his pistol from his belt, motioned to the dog, and moved quickly to the rear of the cabin.

He knelt behind a bush as he listened and looked about the enclave to discern that all was quiet, and then he crouched low and moved to the window at the side of the cabin. He knelt on his knees below the window and could hear voices. When he glanced up at the window, he was pleased to see that the cloth covering had blown back, and he was able to see into the room. He slowly raised his head and looked in.

Hannah stood near the center of the room conversing with a man who held a gun in his hand. LaBerge recognized him as one of the men who had been with Kilkenny, when he and his men had ridden into the settlers camp the night after they had left the flatboat. Hannah's father and a whiskered man stood nearby. Hannah's mother lay on a cot, the blanket pulled up tight about her neck, and her face filled with fear.

The man with the gun stood a few feet apart from the others and LaBerge noticed that the gun was pointed toward the floor and not directly at Hannah or her father. In the silence of the night, LaBerge could easily hear Hannah as she said, "Please, Mr. Keaton, let me take my parents and leave."

Keaton's eyes darted about the small room, and he was silent for a long moment, and then he said, "I . . . I can't. You heard the shot and the scream. Kilkenny's been injured. Turk knifed him in the back.

I'm not sure how bad he's hurt, but I can't abandon him while he's injured, and if I let you go, Kilkenny will kill me. I . . . I can't do it." There was a melancholy in his voice, almost a note of despair and resignation to his fate as he said, "I . . . I think more trouble is brewing. I think the lids about to blow off this place. I'm not sure what I should do? Things are a mess!"

Hannah took a step forward and her face carried a faint smile as she said, "I . . . I think you're probably a pretty good man Mr. Keaton. I think perhaps you fell in with Kilkenny due to circumstances. Why don't you give him and this bad way of life up, and come with us? Leave Kilkenny behind you."

Keaton hesitated again and then said, "I think come tomorrow Kilkenny's gonna need all the help he can get. I think maybe Turk's men will try and kill him. I . . . I couldn't turn again' him just now. Not under these circumstances."

LaBerge ducked down below the window and whispered to the dog, "Stay here Shag. Come through the window if I yell."

He eased his way along the side of the cabin and then to the door. He quickly surveyed the grounds again. He could see no one and all appeared calm and quiet. He stood for a moment at the front door and then he eased the door open and quickly stepped inside, his pistol leveled at Keaton. When the door opened Keaton whirled toward him as LaBerge called out, "Take it easy man, I don't mean you any harm."

Slowly Keaton lowered his gun. "Yer, LaBerge!" he exclaimed.

"Yes, I've come to rescue Hannah and her parents. I heard what Hannah just said to you; inviting you to join us in escaping this prison. Think it over Keaton. I'm willing to help you if you'll agree to come with us."

"I . . . I don't know. I don't think I can. Like I just said; the lids about to blow off this place."

LaBerge said nothing for a moment as he stepped into the cabin and shut the door. He looked at Keaton as he said, "Kilkenny's made his own bed for many years. It's a hard bed he's made for himself, but he'll have to make the best of it. He's not your problem. Give him up."

'I don't know. Perhaps . . ."

Keaton's indecision was cut short as the door was suddenly thrust open and the bulking form of a huge man suddenly appeared in the doorway of the small cabin.

Keaton's face turned pale and filled with fear as he looked at the big man. "Turk! What . . . what are you doing here?" he gasped.

The huge man stood silent as his eyes darted about the room and then his eyes settled on LaBerge. "Who are you? One of my men spotted ya sneakin' across to this cabin. What ya doin' here?"

LaBerge took a step forward as he quickly surveyed this huge, bearded, round--faced man. "The names Jean LaBerge."

"What's your business here? How'd ya get here?"

LaBerge didn't respond immediately to this inquiry as he let his eyes roam over the huge man. What kind of man was he? Was all that he had heard about him true? Would he attempt to prevent him from taking Hannah and her parents and leaving this enclave? Before he could reply a tall, string-bean of a man, with a hawk face and black beard stepped in through the open door and took a place beside Turk. He carried a long rifle in his hands although it wasn't pointed directly at LaBerge or anyone in the room.

LaBerge took note of this new intruder for a moment and concluded he would do nothing unless Turk was threatened. He looked back at the big man and held his voice steady as he said, "This young lady and her family were brought here against their will by Kilkenny, and I've come to take them away. I came down from the overlook above your camp earlier tonight." He paused for a moment as he looked directly into Turk's dark eyes and said in what he hoped

138

was both a firm and friendly voice, "I hope that you will not attempt to hinder me in this mission."

Belle Turk said nothing as he stared at LaBerge. a faint smile on his fat face as he appeared to be taking the measure of the tall, buckskin clad man who stood before him. Turk was a huge, strong man who intimidated most men, and he feared few men, but there was something about this stranger, who stood relaxed, but with firm and steady eyes as he faced him, which told him that he wasn't intimidated or frightened by his size. His smile broadened as he said, "No, I'll not hinder ya in carryin' out your mission. In fact, I'll be right pleased to see the girl and her family gone from here. We'll see you on your way first thing tomorrow," He paused, "I'm glad you came, perhaps you can talk some sense into Kilkenny and get him to leave as well. I'd hoped to kill him, but guess my aim was off a bit. He's in his cabin where Taggert's lookin' after him."

"That's fine by me. I've no quarrel with you. We'll be gone as soon as it's light enough to travel." LaBerge emitted a low chuckle, "But I'll leave Kilkenny here for you to deal with. He's your problem not mine."

"That's fine. I'll deal with Kilkenny. I'm gonna kick him out tomorrow, dead or alive!"

Turk shoved his pistol into his belt as he and his tall companion stepped into the room. His eyes settled on the bearded man who had accompanied Hannah across the enclave. "Who are you? Seems as if the place is crawlin' with strangers."

The man stepped forward as he said, "I'm Jake Herat, I brought the girl back here tonight to rescue her parents." He glanced at LaBerge. "It appears that she has more than one friend who has come to her aid."

"Yeah, it appears so," exclaimed Turk. "Ya can all leave in the morning."

A sudden movement at the door of the cabin caught LaBerge's eye and he looked up to see Kilkenny and Taggart standing in the doorway. Both held guns in their hands. Kilkenny held a pistol and Taggert a long rifle, both were leveled at the big man, Belle Turk.

Every eye in the room turned to the doorway and settled on Kilkenny. He stood slightly hunched over, as if in great pain, and the back and side of his buckskin shirt was soaked in blood. His hard eyes darted about the room, a sneer splashed across his face as he spoke, "I'm not dead Turk. Yeah, yer knife cut me up some, but I can still pull the trigger on this gun and that's what I'm gonna do. I'm gonna send ya to hell, Belle Turk; that's where ya are headed, an' I hope ya burn forever. You tried to kill me and now the tables have turned! I'm gonna kill ya Turk!"

The full meaning of Kilkenny's ejaculation swept through Laberge like a gale force wind. Kilkenny intended to kill Turk and continue to hold Hannah and her family captive. In that moment, the room exploded as everyone understood and reacted to Kilkenny's declaration. Turk clawed for his pistol, the tall hawk-nosed man brought up his long rifle and fired at Kilkenny, and LaBerge dove to his right and shot past the hulk of Belle Turk at Kilkenny. Mrs. Cody and Hannah screamed, as Jedidiah Cody and Herat pushed Hannah up against the side of the cabin and shielded her.

Kilkenny had not expected this explosive reaction and his face suddenly turned white with pain and horror as the bullets from the hawk-nosed man's rifle and from LaBerge's pistol slammed into him, sending him reeling back through the doorway and into the darkness of the night. As he fell, he pulled the trigger on his own pistol, sending the shot into the ceiling of the cabin.

A moment of stunned silence ensued as the sounds of the gunshots filled the cabin and reverberated across the Roost, and then Taggert yelled, "Don't shoot! I give up!"

Turk turned and swept up the lantern from the table and stepped from the cabin to stand over Kilkenny. He looked down at the fallen man with hard eyes as Kilkenny clutched at his chest which was now covered with blood. "I'm not goin' ta hell Kilkenny," Turk spat out. "Least ways not today. But I think ya will be there in a few minutes. Ya will fit in there right well. I'd guess they will have a welcoming party for ya."

Kilkenny tried to raise his head and speak but only a groan and a hiss passed his lips and then his body went limp, and his eyes slowly glassed over. Turk turned and looked at LaBerge and his tall companion. "I believe the two of ya have killed him," he said. "Good riddance!"

Turk motioned them all back into the cabin and he returned the lantern to the table. He stepped toward LaBerge and LaBerge could hear his heavy breathing. And then Turk reached and placed his hand on LaBerge's shoulder as he said, "I'm much obliged to you. The man intended to kill me! I'm beholden to you."

"You owe me nothing," replied LaBerge. "My real aim was to protect this young lady and her family, and I believe this has been accomplished, with the help of your friend."

LaBerge turned from Turk to see Hannah making her way through the smoke-filled room toward him. She came to his side and looked up at him with wide and frightened eyes. She said nothing as she fell against his chest as sobs shook her body. She clung to him for several moments as he held her close and then she lifted her head and looked up at him as she said, "When you stepped through the door of the cabin you were the most wonderful sight in the world!" There was a broad smile across her face as she continued, "I'd kiss you if there weren't so many people around."

CHAPTER 18

Rescued

The gunsmoke drifted slowly out the open door and through the windows of the cabin and dissipated into the night. LaBerge released Hannah and stepped to the window and called to his dog. "Hop on in Shag, everything seems to be in control now." He was introduced to the hermit, Jake Herat and then LaBerge, Keaton, and Herat carried the body of Kilkenny to his cabin and laid him on his cot. Turk followed them into the cabin and then stood, looking down on the still, pale, and bloody corpse for a long moment and then looked up as he said, "My men and I will bury him tomorrow." His face carried a sober expression as he looked at LaBerge. "A few other men have died here over the past few years and there's a small cemetery at the back of the property." The big man chuckled, "There's plenty of room for him."

When they left Kilkenny's cabin Herat turned to LaBerge. "You go to the girl's cabin." A sly smile filled his face as he looked at LaBerge. "I suspect she would like to spend some time alone with you and has a few things to say to you."

"Yes, I'll go to her and have her go with me to retrieve my horse. He's probably wondering what has happened to me." LaBerge reached and slapped Herat on the shoulder as he said, "I want to thank you for coming here this evening with Hannah to rescue her parents. It was mighty nice of you to agree to help her, especially since she was a stranger to you."

142

Herat laughed, "Well, to tell you the truth, Mr. LaBerge, I only came because she badgered me into coming. I was of the opinion that it was a fool's errand that might get us both killed."

"I understand, and all the more reason to thank you. I'm pleased that, except for Kilkenny, things have turned out very well and we can all leave in the morning."

"Yeah, it turns out this guy Turk is not as bad as his reputation."

Herat looked across the dark yard at Cody's wagon for a long moment. "I'd guess it was mighty tough getting that contraption up here. The girl and I brought along a couple of extra horses for her parents to ride on. We can leave the wagon here." He paused as he looked across the enclave toward the stand of trees the two of them had waited in before making their way to the cabin. "The horses are tied up back of the trees. I'll go fetch them."

When LaBerge appeared at the front of the cabin, Hannah and her father were standing just outside the door. When Jedidiah spotted him, he rushed forward and embraced LaBerge in a bear hug. He stepped back as he exclaimed, "How does a man say, 'THANK YOU' when he owes so much, but thank you for coming to our rescue."

LaBerge started to reply but before he could say anything. Jedidiah said. "I'm going in and go to bed. It's been an eventful night!" He gestured toward his daughter. "I have an idea that the two of you would like to exchange a few words." He looked up at the dark sky and chuckled, "I was about to say, 'don't stay out too late,' but it must be after two o'clock so that doesn't make any sense." He chuckled again and then opened the door and entered the cabin.

When the door to the cabin closed, they stood looking at each other for a long moment and then he stepped forward and took her hand as he said, "It was very brave of you to escape from this place and then come back with Herat in an attempt to rescue your parents." He glanced at her arms and legs as he said, "I can't see much here in the dark, but earlier, when we were in the cabin, I believe I saw that your arms were scratched and bruised, and I saw a red welt on the side of your head. You must have had a rough time making your way down the mountain."

The Roost was encased in heavy darkness, but the light of a pale half-moon played across her long hair as she said, "Yes, it was very dark when I escaped, and I fell several times as I made my way down the mountain. And then the next morning I stumbled at what was a very steep precipice and tumbled down the mountain and hit my head on a rock. Mr. Herat heard me scream and came and found me. He didn't much want to, but he finally agreed to come back with me to help rescue my parents, but I'm sure happy that you were here when Kilkenny came to the cabin with his gun. He intended to kill Turk and then keep us captive. He . . . he was a wicked man!"

"Yes, I'm glad I was here when Kilkenny appeared in the door of the cabin, but it's all behind us now. We'll leave in the morning and you, and your parent's will be shut of this place."

"Yes, I hate this place and will be glad to leave it."

Hannah took a small step forward and stood very near to LaBerge as she looked up at him. The light from the moon illuminated his chiseled face and she was sure that he was the most handsome and brave man she had ever met. She rose up on her toes as she said, "Mr. LaBerge, I'm going to give you that kiss I promised you an hour ago in the cabin. Do you mind?"

He gazed down into her shinning eyes as he thought; *No man in his right mind would refuse such an offer,* and then he murmured, "No . . . no, I don't mind. In fact, I'm looking forward to it." And then before she could reply he swept her up into his arms and kissed her on the lips. The kiss lingered for a long moment as an owl looked down from a tree and then hooted at the embracing couple.

When the kiss finally came to an end, he held her close as he whispered. "Hannah, when we are away from here, and have traveled to Blue Valley, I have a very important question that I intend to ask you, but I don't believe that now is the time for me to bring the matter up."

She stepped back and looked up at him and the pale moonlight cast a soft glow across her face as she said, "I . . . I hope it's the question I'm thinking of, and I know what my answer will be."

He took her hand as he said, "I'm happy to hear that. Let's give it some time to grow and mature." He tugged on her hand as he said, "Will you come with me to get my horse. I'd like that."

She squeezed his hand as she said, "Yes, I'd like to go with you." She smiled up at him in the darkness as she laughed. "Pa and Ma are asleep, but I do have my knife to protect myself." She laughed again. "But I'd never use it on you Mr. LaBerge. You've already kissed me tonight, so it's too late to pull my knife on you, and besides, I liked the kiss!"

*****

It was late morning, before they left the Roost. Hannah's father had made a deal with Belle Turk to swap the oxen and wagon for two pack mules. LaBerge assisted Jedidiah in preparing the mule packs. Hannah's father had retrieved the carpet bag, containing his money, from where he had hidden it in the bed of the wagon and carefully stowed it in one of the mule packs.

Early that morning LaBerge had taken Hannah's father aside and told him about Grace Growden Galloway and his obligation to her. "I promised her I would return and escort her to her sister's home. I would be pleased if you, your wife, and Hannah would come with me to fetch her and then we'll all go on together."

"Yes, I understand," Jedidiah had replied, "If you will consent, I would very much like for you to then accompany my family on to our destination at Olive Hill. I'll not venture out into this frontier wilderness alone again. I've learned my lesson."

"Yes, of course, I'll be happy to see you safely on to your final destination." LaBerge had paused for a moment and placed his hand on Hannah's father's shoulder, a broad smile across his face as he said, "Mr. Cody, I must tell you that I intend to court your daughter and will most likely ask her to marry me and make her home with me in Blue Valley."

Jedidiah had looked up at the tall man with a sly smile on his face as he said, "I'm not surprised, and nothing would please mc more than to have you as a son-in-law. We'll cross the bridge about going on to Olive Hill later."

While LaBerge and Jedidiah had been packing the mule packs the big man, Belle Turk, had pulled LaBerge aside and said to him, "I don't want ya to leave here with the wrong impression of me and my men, who spend a good deal of time here at what I call the Roost." There was a sly grin on his fat face as he looked at Laberge. "I'm sure you have observed that we're not all lily-white and without fault, and that includes myself. However, we're not the black cutthroats that some have made us out to be. Sure, most of us have had our scrapes with the law and a few men are here in an effort to escape the long arm of the law from back east. And I'm somewhat ashamed to say that a couple of the men are deserters from the army and one man is a deserter from the Red Coats, so I guess it sort of balances out. As I said, we're not lily white, but we're not a bunch of cut-throat thieves, lying in wait for travelers to rob and murder. I guess you could say we're a bunch of miss-fits. We mostly hunt, fish, gamble, and loaf. I guess it would be fair to say were a lazy bunch of men."

LaBerge had not hesitated as he had replied, "I didn't come here to interfere with you and your men. I came only to rescue the girl and her parents from Kilkenny. He's dead now, and we'll be on our way. I'll leave it to others to deal with any lawbreakers here in the Roost." He held out his hand to Turk as they parted, "Thank you for not standing in the way of our leaving this place." LaBerge paused for a long moment as he looked at Belle Turk and when he spoke there was a sly grin on his face as he said, "I'm pleased that we avoided a clash, but I would have taken you on, if necessary, to rescue the girl."

Belle Turk stepped back a step as a grin spread across his fat face. "LaBerge," he exclaimed, "I've always enjoyed a good fight, but

O. L. Brown

I'm thinking maybe this is one fight I'm better off to have avoided. Ha! Ha! Ha!" he laughed, "I think maybe I would have had my hands full." He waved his arm toward the trail that led from the Roost as he said, "Be on yer way young man!" There was even a twinkle in his eyes as he said, "And you treat that young lady right or I *will* come and take ya on. Ha! Ha!"

With Hannah riding at his side LaBerge led the little caravan when it left the Roost, with one of the pack mules trotting along behind LaBerge's horse. Hannah's parents followed along behind them with a line trailing to the second pack mule. Keaton and Taggert rode behind Hannah's parents, with the hermit, Herat, bringing up the rear of the group.

As they were preparing to leave the Roost, Herat had said, "I think we can make it to my cabin today and you can all spend the night there."

CHAPTER 19

Kidnapped

T hey were gone this morning," exclaimed the innkeeper, an exasperated look spread across his face as he looked up at the tall figure of Jean LaBerge. "I was very surprised to find that Mrs. Galloway and her attendant, James, had left sometime during the night, especially since James was still recovering from his gunshot wound." The innkeeper paused in his explanation, and then continued, his voice filled with agitation. "And she didn't even pay her bill! But I think that . . .."

LaBerge interrupted, "Did anyone see them leave?"

"Yes," exclaimed the innkeeper. "Frenchie's cow had gotten out of the corral sometime during the night. He said he heard the cow stomping about in the yard and had gotten out of bed and gone out to put her back into the corral. He said it was about five in the morning and just starting to show a hint of daylight and when he looked up from shutting the corral gate, he saw Mrs. Galloway, Mr. Patterson, and two other men riding north out of the settlement."

"Did you see that man, Swingate Calvert, after I left here last week? Did he come back?"

"Yeah, I seen him. He was back here in the settlement the next day after ya left, an' I seen him a talkin' to Mrs. Galloway a couple of times and I could see that she was none too happy with the man."

"Thanks," said LaBerge. "How much did Mrs. Galloway owe you for the two rooms?"

"Two and a half dollars." His eyes lit up. "Ya gonna pay me what she owned me?"

"Yes, I'll take care of her bill." LaBerge took out his leather bag and counted out the money in coins and then turned from the man.

LaBerge had taken only a couple of steps when the innkeeper called out, "Wait! I almost forgot. I found this envelope addressed to you under Mrs. Galloway's pillow when I was cleanin' up the room the next morning after she left." He handed LaBerge a sealed envelope as he said, "As ya can see, it's addressed to you, so I didn't open it."

LaBerge looked down at the envelope as he walked toward the door of the inn. His name was scrawled across the face of the envelope. Considering the rather poor nature of the handwriting it appeared to have been written in hast.

Hannah walked beside him as they left the inn. She looked down at the envelope that LaBerge held in his hands as she exclaimed. "I wonder what this Mrs. Galloway has written to you?"

LaBerge ducked as they stepped through the door and into the bright sunshine. "We'll find out," he said as he tore the envelope open. He took out a small piece of paper and held it so that Hannah could see the note as he quickly scanned the scrawled handwriting. He didn't know Mrs. Galloway's handwriting but guessed that her penmanship was usually much better than the writing on this paper.

Mr. LaBerge. Calvert has returned and is forcibly taking James and me back to my old home in Bensalem, Pennsylvania. I have gained a moment of privacy by telling him that I must change into clothing more suitable for traveling. Please come to my aid as soon as possible. He has not disclosed his proposed route, but I believe it is probable that he will take us by riverboat as far as Pittsburg, or perhaps a little beyond. I will die before I sign the deeds.

Grace Growden Galloway

P. S. I'll try and leave some kind of a sign along the way to guide you.

He looked up from the note and said nothing for a long moment as his eyes swept across the dirt street and up at the silent, green hills. The hills seemed to speak of peace and beauty but the note from Mrs. Galloway spoke sharply of treachery and deceit. A deep anger began to well up in the gut of the tall man. Anger that Calvert had returned and had kidnapped Mrs. Galloway. Yes, he would go and rescue her.

Hannah intruded upon his thoughts as she exclaimed, "What are you going to do? Are you going to try and rescue her?"

He didn't reply immediately to her inquiry as he quickly scanned the note again, as if to make sure he fully understood what had happened to Mrs. Galloway. He turned to Hannah as he said, "Yes, I must go immediately and rescue her from this man, Calvert. As you can see from her note, he is taking her back to Pennsylvania and is going to attempt to force her to sign the deeds conveying all of her property to him. I can't let that happen. I must help her."

Hannah looked up at him. "How . . . how will you find her?"

"I believe it likely they will travel north along the Big Sandy River until they come to Huntington on the Ohio River, where they can board a flatboat going northeast to Pittsburg." He hesitated for a moment as he gathered his thoughts. "They have a little over a day's head start on me, but Calvert won't make good time with Mrs. Galloway and the injured James Patterson in tow. Mrs. Galloway is a resourceful woman and I suspect she'll endeavor to slow their progress as much as possible, so perhaps I can overtake them before they board the flatboat."

Hannah looked up at him, her eyes filled with alarm. I . . . I wish you didn't have to go, but I understand."

"Yes, I must find her and rescue her from this man." He looked down into Hannah's sad and downcast eyes as he continued, "I'm sorry to have to leave you and your parents, but I must go. As soon as I can gather some grub I'm going to leave. I'll push my horse and travel through the night. Hopefully, I can overtake them before they board the flatboat."

Hannah stepped close to the tall man and the sadness now left her face as she looked up at him. "I'll pray that you find this lady and her attendant." She paused for a moment as she looked up at him. "I'd like to go with you and help find the lady. Will you let me come with you?"

He said nothing as he shifted his eyes up toward the blue hillsides that rose up above the settlement. His heart and mind were fighting a raging battle over her request. The thought of leaving her again nearly tore him apart. The battle didn't rage long, and his mind won as he said, "No, it may be dangerous. It's best for you to remain here with your parents and assist them."

"Yes, I suppose so," she replied, with a crestfallen look on her face. "But I wish that I could go with you." She looked up into his face as she continued, "I . . . I don't want to be separated from you again and you're going to rescue this lady and her assistant frighten me, Jean. You could be injured or killed! I wish you had someone to go with you to help you."

LaBerge said nothing as he folded the note, slid it back into the envelope, and pushed it into his shirt pocket. "Come with me," he said as he took her arm and walked with her a few paces to the corner of the building and led her into the shadows of the building and away from prying eyes. He looked down into her questioning face as he said, "I'll come back Hannah. I'll come back and then we'll all travel on to Blue Valley. I'd consider taking you with me, but it wouldn't be proper for you to travel alone with me, and I may encounter a very dangerous situation, and I wouldn't want you to be

151

hurt or killed. I couldn't live with myself if something were to happen to you."

He thought he detected the mist of a tear in her eyes as she said, "I . . . I understand. I'll be here Jean, waiting for you when you return. I hope it won't be too long."

They stood in the shadowed corner of the building, but the setting was far from romantic with people, horses, carts and wagons traversing along the street only a few feet away, but sometimes you followed your heart, regardless of the circumstances, and with a tenderness of love in his eyes he swept her up into his arms and kissed her. When the kiss was at an end, she clung to him as she laid her head on his shoulder and then said in a soft voice, "I've fallen in love with you Jean! Please come back. Please come back to me."

As he held her close, he glanced out along the street. A street that was busy with the day-to-day activities of frontier people going about their daily business. The voices of people, the rumble of wagons, and the snorting of animals filled the air. Where they stood was anything but a romantic spot, but he would not let the people and the noise of the moment deter him from what his heart told him he must do.

He held her at arms-length as he looked down into her eyes. Eyes that he could see were filled with fear, hope, and love. His voice was barely above a whisper as he said, "Hannah, this isn't a very romantic setting, and I had intended to postpone asking you this question until we had arrived in Blue Valley, but I'm going to ask you now, before I leave to go and rescue Mrs. Galloway. Perhaps it will make things easier for both of us if I pose the question now, before we are parted again." He fell silent as he drew her close and his voice was filled with a dreamy pathos as he said, "Hannah, when I come back from rescuing Mrs. Galloway, will you marry me and live with me in Blue Valley?"

They stood in the shadow of the building and no sunlight played across her face, but despite this absence of bright light, he could see the sparkle in her eyes and hear the lilt in her voice as she pulled herself close to him again and her arms entwined his neck as she whispered. "Yes Jean, I'll marry you when you return. I would like to be your wife" She looked up at him, with a mixture of tears in her eyes and a smile on her face, as she whispered, "Come back soon Jean. Come back and we will be married."

"Yes, I'll come back Hannah and we'll go to Blue Valley and then we'll be married."

She fell against him as she looked up into his face. "Yes," she whispered. "We will be married in Blue Valley."

He looked across the street to where her parents stood under a shade tree. "I need to tell your father that I must go and rescue Mrs. Galloway and that you and your parents will need to remain here for a few days, and then I must be on my way."

He took her arm, and they walked across the street toward her parents.

CHAPTER 20

The Chase

J ean LaBerge tugged his slicker uptight about his neck as he
hunched his shoulders against the cold, driving, wind and rain.
The rain had come during the night, and, except for a few
intermittent gaps, it had rained throughout the day as he had pushed
his horse north along the Big Sandy River. He had ridden hard since
leaving Williamson yesterday afternoon, pausing for only a few hours
during the middle of the night at a small stable where he had fed his
horse, had kicked up a bit of straw for a bed, and had dozed fitfully
for a couple of hours.

It was still dark when he had saddled his horse and had ridden
back out into the cold and rain. An hour later a gray, wet dawn had
come reluctantly to the rain shrouded hills. He had paused only long
enough to grab a quick breakfast of eggs and ham at a small tavern
that lay next to the river. When he had inquired of the tavern owner,
the man had told him that two men, a middle-aged lady, of obvious
refinement, and a man, who appeared to be in considerable distress,
had stopped at the tavern yesterday for a late lunch and had then
pushed on north along the river. "I don't know where they planned to
spend the night, perhaps at the small settlement of Louisa. There is
a fair size tavern and inn there. Perhaps they stopped there for the
night."

His hurried breakfast behind him, he had ridden back out into the rain and wind. Based on the comments of the tavern keeper he was confident that Calvert was taking Mrs. Galloway and James to Huntington where they would board the riverboat. His spirits had been further bolstered when he had spotted a small white handkerchief fluttering from a bush. He was sure the handkerchief belonged to Mrs. Galloway as the initials GGG had been embroidered in the corner of the handkerchief. He had smiled to himself; Mrs. Galloway had left him a sign telling him he was on the right trail.

He cocked his head down against the wind in an effort to ward off some of the rain. He continued to push on even though he was tired and worn to a frazzle from the hard and relentless pace he had maintained since leaving Williamson yesterday. He glanced down at his dog, Shag, who trudged along beside his horse, his tongue hanging out the side of his mouth. He suspected that both dog and horse were as tired and worn as he was.

Over the course of the next half hour, he passed three log cabins, suggesting that he was nearing the settlement of Louisa, and within a few minutes he topped a small rise where he reined in his horse and looked down on the log cabins and rough buildings of the settlement, which lay scattered haphazardly along the banks of the river. He descended the knoll and rode into the edge of the settlement where he paused again. Ahead of him, along a muddy street, he could see a sign advertising the BIG SANDY TAVERN AND INN. Perhaps he could learn more about how far Calvert and his hostages were ahead of him from the owner of the tavern. He touched his heels to his horse and moved on towards the tavern.

He was still a hundred yards shy of the tavern when he glanced to his right along a side street, almost an alley, and was surprised to see what appeared to be Mrs. Galloway's appaloosa horse, as well as two other horses hitched to a railing. He quickly reined in his horse and surveyed the narrow side street and the horses. *Was it possible? Had he caught up with Calvert and his hostages? And what were they doing here on this small side street?*

He quickly turned his horse and rode back to the edge of the settlement. He tied his horse to a tree and taking only his pistol, which he tucked in below his belt, he turned to the dog. "Come on, Shag, let's check this out."

He returned to the side street and surveyed the three horses, all standing patiently, with heads down, against the incessant rain. He believed the appaloosa horse was Mrs. Galloway's mount, and he thought the sorrel was James' horse. He had never seen the big black horse before. Based on what he had been told by the innkeeper at Williamson there should be four horses. He didn't believe the black belonged to Calvert. Where was he and who was the owner of the black?

The narrow street was empty except for the horses. He carefully approached the horses and immediately noticed a dark streak of what appeared to be blood, splotched across the saddle of the sorrel, which he believed belonged to James. This suggested that James was experiencing trouble in traveling, confirming what the man at the tavern had suggested to him earlier today. He looked up and surveyed the adjacent buildings and immediately saw a small sign: DR. RALPH PICKTON, above a doorway. To the right of the doorway was a small window. He stepped to the window and was startled to see Mrs. Galloway seated in the room with her back to the window.

He stepped away from the window as he considered his next move. He doubted if Calvert was in the doctor's office, but it was likely that his accomplice was. However, he had never seen the man, and consequently, the man would not recognize him either. He turned to his dog. "Wait here," he said.

He pushed the door to the doctor's office open, and without pausing or looking about the small room, he strode across to a desk where a lady sat. "I have a friend who needs to see the doctor," he said to the lady. "When can I bring him in?"

The lady looked up at him as she said, "You can't bring him in now as the doctor is presently engaged in treating a man who has been seriously injured, so it may be an hour or two before he is free to see your friend. Perhaps you could come back later."

"I see. Yes, that will be fine. I'll return later." He turned and as he stepped away from the woman his eyes locked on Mrs. Galloway for only an instant, but in that moment, he saw relief in her eyes. As he looked away, she made an almost imperceptible nod of her head toward a tall man, dressed in black breeches and a dark tricorne hat, who was seated in a chair a few feet from her. That nod told him that this was Calvert's accomplice. He made a quick glance at the tall man as he strode to the door. The man's eyes were cast down at the floor, in apparent boredom, and he took no notice of LaBerge. The man didn't appear to have a weapon, but it was possible that his coat concealed a pistol tucked into an inside pocket. Beyond that quick observation he could tell little of what to expect from the man when the inevitable confrontation came.

He stepped from the doctor's office and spoke to his dog, who had curled up next to the building. "Come boy, we've got some more sleuthing to do." As he stepped back to the street, he noted that the rain had slackened to a light drizzle. When he looked west, he was pleased to see that the clouds had begun to lighten. Perhaps the rain would cease shortly. He paused at the street and looked toward the tavern. Several horses and a couple of donkeys stood in front of the dark building. Perhaps Calvert was in the tavern. He'd start his search for the man there.

When he approached the tavern, he carefully surveyed the horses. He couldn't be sure, but he felt that the light dune mare was probably the horse that Calvert had been riding when he had escorted him out of Williamson a few days past. He turned from the horses and said to the dog. "Stay here, I'll yell if I need you." Shag sniffed about the side of the tavern for a moment and then lay down in the shelter of the wall.

LaBerge paused at the door and unbuttoned the three sides of his hat, allowing the brim to sag about his face, giving him the look of a back-country hick. In addition, he pulled the collar of his slicker up tight, about his neck and face, and deliberately slouched his shoulders. He didn't think Calvert would immediately recognize him.

He pushed the door to the tavern open, and ducked his head as he stepped inside. He stood for a moment as he took in the small room. Two men, neither of them Calvert, were seated at a table as they spoke in low tones and sipped tankards of ale. A fat, whiskered man, that he took to be the owner, stood behind a low bench, with an apron wrapped about his waist, as he conversed with a man who stood leaning against the bench. He could see no one else in the room. *Where was Calvert? He must be in one of the back rooms of the tavern. Did Calvert know someone here in this small settlement? Perhaps someone who would help him if he needed assistance?*

LaBerge lingered just inside the door for a few moments as he continued to look about the room and then he approached the man behind the counter. Would this man be helpful, or would he attempt to hinder him in finding Calvert?

The man nodded his head at LaBerge as he approached. "How can I help you sir?" He nodded his head toward the door as he continued, "It's a bad day and ya look as if ya have been out in the weather some."

"Yes, the rain is tiresome," responded LaBerge. He smiled at the man. "But I see some clearing in the west, so perhaps it will improve as the day wears on."

The man grinned at LaBerge as he said, "I'll get ya a tankard of ale. That'll warm ya up a bit and help dry ya out."

LaBerge waited at the bench while the man was away. Out of long habit of vigilance his eyes roamed the room, noting the movements of the patrons and watching for Calvert to emerge from one of the two doors he could see: one on the side and the other at the rear of the room. The man set the tankard of ale on the bench as he said, "Here ya are. I hope it goes down well."

LaBerge took a drink from the tankard of ale and set it back down on the bench. His voice was low as he said, "I'm looking for a man; a short, heavy man. I believe the dune mare tethered outside may be his, but I don't see him here in the tavern."

The aproned man's eyes suddenly clouded as he looked across the bench at LaBerge. He said nothing for a long moment and then he said, "Are ya huntin' him as a friend or foe? He's got friends here and he can be a dangerous man if ya get on the wrong side of him."

LaBerge's voice was calm as he said, "That all depends upon Mr. Calvert. I'll not cause him any trouble if he releases the man and woman, he is holding hostage, but if he refuses then things may get a little rough."

The aproned innkeeper looked across the bench at LaBerge and his voice was barely above a whisper as he said, "It's yer fight, but take it out of my tavern, I don't want my place to be . . .."

CHAPTER 21

The Fight

The comments of the tavern keeper were interrupted by a sudden commotion of loud voices as four men walked boisterously through the side door and into the room. Laberge looked up to see Calvert and his rough looking companions make their way to a table where they grabbed chairs and seated themselves. Their conversation continued in animated outbursts of rough talk and raucous laughter.

LaBerge immediately pulled his hat down lower over his forehead as he watched the foursome. Anger welled up in his gut when he heard Calvert mention Mrs. Galloway in an offhand and derisive manner. Within a few minutes one of the men turned from the rowdy conversation and directed his attention across the room to the man in the apron, as he called out in a loud voice, "Hey man, fetch us some ale and crackers. We need somethin' ta munch on and to wet our whistles! Shake a leg, man!"

The tavern owner was slow in responding as he stared at the men at the table, his face filled with a touch of fear and then he called out, "I'll be along in a moment." He glanced at LaBerge as he mumbled in a low tone, "There's yer man and his friends. I'd be mighty careful if I were you. They're a hard lot, especially when they've had a bit too much ta drink."

LaBerge continued to stand at the bench as he watched the drinks and crackers being delivered to the four men. Calvert hadn't recognized him, but probably would, if he approached the table. The men took their drinks and resumed their animated banter.

As he watched the men and heard their babble, he began to consider his next move. He would need to move with care and subterfuge. He couldn't directly take on these four men without risk of serious injury or even death, and neither outcome would deliver Mrs. Galloway from her captivity. He needed to separate Calvert from his friends. One on one, he wasn't afraid of the outcome with Calvert. He laid a coin on the bench and said to the tavernkeeper in a low voice, "Here's payment for the drink. I'm going to step outside." He nodded toward the men at the table. "In a few minutes will you tell Calvert that he's wanted at the doctor's office located in the side-street just down the street."

The apron clad man said nothing for a moment as he glanced from LaBerge to Calvert and his companions and then back. There was a touch of fear in his eyes as he looked across the bench at LaBerge. "Yes . . . yes, I'll tell him."

LaBerge made his way out of the tavern, walked a few steps, and then paused. He noted that the rain had almost ceased, and when he looked west above the gray hills, he could see a faint blue in the far western sky. His dog, Shag, had jumped to his feet and looked at him with questioning eyes that seemed to indicate his pleasure that he had returned. "Come boy," said LaBerge, and the dog fell in behind him as he made his way along the muddy street in the direction of the doctor's office.

When he came to the side-street where the doctor's office was located, he found that nothing had changed since he had left a half hour ago. The three horses continued to stand at the hitching rail, their heads down in boredom, as they swished their tails to ward off flies. He slipped past the horses and took a position behind several empty wooden ale barrels and some boxes that were stacked along the far end of the alley and next to the building. He motioned to a spot behind a box as he said to his dog, "Lay down here Shag. Don't move unless I yell." The dog immediately crouched down behind the box but remained alert. LaBerge pulled up a box and sat down behind a barrel. He took off his hat, rebuttoned the three sides and then returned it to his head.

He hoped that Calvert would be alone when he came, but if his three companions were with him, he knew he faced a challenging dilemma. In addition, Calvert had a friend in the doctor's office, and it could be five against one, very poor odds. The dog would help to even the odds, but probably not enough. If Calvert was alone then he only had two men to deal with. He felt that he could handle those odds.

The rain had now ceased, and LaBerge shucked off his slicker, so as to give him better freedom of movement. He gave his full attention to the street at the end of the alley, anticipating the arrival of Calvert within a few minutes. A heavy silence lay along the alley; the only sounds being the movement of the three horses and the creaking of their leather saddles. The faint bawl of a calf drifted in from some distance away, and he heard a man as he shouted out to someone. The silence continued for several minutes and LaBerge was beginning to doubt if Calvert was going to come and then the rotund man suddenly strode into view at the head of the alley. He stopped and looked at the horses and then along the alley, his eyes darting about the narrow street.

LaBerge hesitated in his hiding place. It seemed as if Calvert was expecting to see someone, and then Calvert turned as if to enter the doctor's office. LaBerge rose from behind the barrels and called out, "Calvert, do you remember what I told you when we parted after I had escorted you from the settlement of Williamson?"

Calvert whirled and his eyes took on a dark hardness as he said, "Yeah, I remember, but it ain't gonna turn out the way ya expect."

As LaBerge stepped away from the barrels he pulled his pistol from his belt. He hoped the pistol in his hand would discourage Calvert from resistance. He took a step forward as he said, "I'm taking Mrs. Galloway and James with me when I leave here. If you resist, I'll do whatever is necessary to accomplish my mission, and that includes killing you if I have to."

A snicker filled the round face of the man as he looked along the alley at LaBerge and LaBerge could see that his eyes had glanced beyond him. And then LaBerge heard a sound from the far end of the alley, and he knew he was trapped. He was pretty sure that when he turned, he would see Calvert's three friends from the tavern behind him. He had made a foolish mistake and it was going to be difficult to overcome these odds. He would get some help from his dog, but he needed more.

Calvert's snicker broke out into a low laugh as he said, "We got ya, LaBerge. Ya can go without the woman, but otherwise it's most likely yer funeral."

LaBerge's next moves were lightning fast. He yelled at his dog, "Get him boy!" as he dived into the barrels behind him, sending them cascading back along the alley and into the men approaching from his rear.

As he sprang back to his feet, he was pleased to see that one man was down from the force of a barrel slamming into him, and the other two men were attempting to evade rolling barrels. As one of the men sidestepped a cascading barrel, he started to bring up his long rifle and LaBerge fired his pistol sending the man reeling back into the mud of the alley.

From behind him LaBerge could hear the snarls of his dog and Calvert's oaths, and then above the din he heard a man call from the doorway to the doctor's office. "Swingate, what's going on out here?" This was undoubtedly Calvert's confederate he had seen in the doctor's office. LaBerge had no time to deal with this new threat as he rushed the man closest to him. He hit the man hard as he drove his shoulder into him, knocking him to the ground. LaBerge quickly regained his feet and was delivering a hard blow across the man's face with his right fist when the man's companion hit him hard from behind, knocking him sprawling into the mud of the alley.

The two men both jump on him with the intention of pinning him to the ground, but LaBerge's powerful thrusts with his arms and legs shoved the men aside, sending one man sprawling into the mud.

LaBerge was on his feet in an instant and he lunged at the man who remained on his feet, driving his shoulder into the man's gut, sending him down onto his back. But before he could turn, he was hit from behind by the second man as he lunged at him, and LaBerge was sent smashing into the mud of the alley again, and now both men were on him as they pummeled him with their fists.

In the melee, he caught a glimpse of his dog biting and snarling at Calvert who lay in the mud of the alley, but what frightened him the most was the gun in the hand of Calvert's companion who stood in the door of the doctor's office. This man, if he could get a clear shot could shoot either LaBerge or his dog; The thought of his dog, Shag, being killed troubled him more than his own possible fate.

The odds were now overwhelming against him, but he would fight on. That was the nature of the tall man from Vermont; he would never give up; perhaps help would come from an unexpected quarter. He would keep fighting as long as he had breath in him.

As he kicked hard at his two attackers and tried to ward off their blows, a vision of a willowy girl, her face shrouded in a bonnet as she smiled up at him, flashed through his mind. *Would he ever see her again?*

With a mighty plowman's thrust of his arms and legs he heaved the two men from him and was on his feet and facing the men as they circled to attack him again. From the corner of his eye, he caught a fleeting glimpse of Mrs. Galloway as she brought her parasol down hard across the head of Calvert's confederate, sending him sprawling out into the alley. This action brought a quick and faint smile to his face.

The man he had shot sat in the mud as he looked about with a dazed look on his face. He was out of the fight. The two men continued to circle LaBerge, looking for a good opening to take him down. They moved with caution as they had learned that this tall stranger was a fighter. And then suddenly the shouts of two men rang out from the entrance to the alley. "Stop it! Let that man go or we'll shoot!"

The men, circling LaBerge, stopped in mid step, as they turned toward the voices. LaBerge's hat was gone, his hair was disheveled, and his clothing covered in mud as he glanced toward the voices, and relief flooded through him as he recognized Taggert and Keaton standing at the head of the alley, each with a pistol in his hand. And then Keaton yelled again, "Stop it, or someone is gonna get killed!"

Taggert advanced into the alley as he said, "You men all line up against the building. LaBerge turned to his dog, who continued to hold Calvert on the ground. "Let him up Shag," he said. With some reluctance the big dog backed away. Calvert slowly pulled himself to his feet and stood glaring at LaBerge and then at Taggert, as he wiped blood from his face and arms. He remained silent as he shuffled up against the wall, his clothing torn, muddy, and covered with blood.

Calvert's confederate heaved himself up out of the mud and onto his feet, shook his head and stared at Mrs. Galloway, his eyes filled with shock and surprise. "You hit me with your parasol!" he exclaimed. "That wasn't very ladylike!"

"Yes, and I'd do it again," exclaimed Mrs. Galloway. "You have no one to blame but yourself; taking up with the likes of Swingate Calvert."

He shook his head in disbelief and then walked to the wall where he made a futile effort to wipe the worst of the mud from his fine clothing.

LaBerge frisked each of the men and took their pistols, rifles, and knives from them. He went to Calvert and looked at him with all of the seriousness he could muster as he said, "You and your men have and hour to leave the settlement. I'm taking Mrs. Galloway and Mr.

Patterson with me when I leave. Don't attempt to interfere with me again!"

LaBerge grabbed up the reins of Calvert's companions' horse and handed them to the man. "Take your horse with you and leave with Calvert."

Calvert turned from the wall and looked at LaBerge with hard eyes as he said, "You're a stubborn and persistent cuss, over an old lady that was against the fight for independence. I don't understand you?"

LaBerge's voice was firm but not harsh. "No, I don't suppose you do. We operate on different values."

Calvert shook his head and motioned to his companions, and they walked slowly to the street and turned toward the tavern. LaBerge, Keaton, Taggart, and Mrs. Galloway watched, as the men shambled along the street. The man LaBerge had shot walked between two men who supported him with their arms wrapped about his shoulders and waist.

Mrs. Galloway turned to LaBerge as she said, "When you walked into the doctor's office nearly an hour ago, I knew you were an angel, sent directly by the Lord to save me!" She stepped forward and grabbed him in a hug. "Thank you, Mr. LaBerge!" she exclaimed. "Thank you for coming to the assistance of this old Loyalist. You are a special man; you are one of a kind!"

She glanced at the two men, Taggart and Keaton, as she continued, "And who are these companion angels?"

LaBerge introduced Taggart and Keaton to Mrs. Galloway, as friends he had only recently met while rescuing Hannah Cody. "I didn't know they were going to follow me here today and come to my assistance, but I sure appreciate it."

LaBerge stepped to Taggert and Keaton and shook their hands as he said, "When I heard your voices it was the most welcome sound I've heard in years. Those guys had me between a rock and a hard place. Things didn't look too good for me."

Keaton shrugged his shoulders as he grinned at LaBerge. "Ah man, I'm guessin' that between you, the dog, and the lady here, that you would have whipped those men. Ha! . . . Ha!"

"Well, perhaps so, but I'm mighty glad the two of you arrived when you did." LaBerge paused for a moment as he looked at the two men. "Why *are* the two of you here in Louisa?"

"There was a gleam of mischief in Keaton's eyes as he said, "It was that girl of yours, Hannah Cody." He looked up at LaBerge with a grin on his face as he said, "That young lady is some stuck on you. You hadn't been gone more than a couple of hours when she came to us and insisted that we leave immediately and try and catch up with you. She said she had been worried sick ever since you had left. She was sure you would need help in rescuing Mrs. Galloway. Well, Taggert and me; we had about decided that we were gonna head back east to where we have relatives and friends, so we agreed to come on and try and catch up with ya. So, while we saddled up, she had the cook at the inn fix us each a bag of food and then we lit out and rode hard most all night."

He laughed. "And it *is* uncanny how we rode into the settlement and found you in a fight here in this alley. Looks like we caught up with ya at about the right time."

"Yes, the timing couldn't have been better," exclaimed LaBerge. "Your help is appreciated."

Mrs. Galloway turned to LaBerge, and her eyes were now clouded and filled with anger as she said, "James Patterson is dead. The forced ride from Williamson was too much for him. Calvert killed him! We will need to find a suitable place to bury him."

CHAPTER 22

Compassion

L aBerge brushed the worst of the mud and grime of the alley from his shirt and pants and then accompanied Mrs. Galloway into the doctor's office. The doctor ushered them into his examination room and the three of them stood in silence as they looked down on the still face of James Patterson. "He was a good man," said Mrs. Galloway, her voice trembling with emotion and her eyes filled with tears.

The doctor led them to his small office and directed Mrs. Galloway to a chair. LaBerge remained standing. The doctor's face carried a sad countenance as he said, "I'm terribly sorry about the death of Mr. Patterson. The hard ride caused his wound to open and by the time you brought him in to me he had lost so much blood that I wasn't able to save him. I'm very sorry Mrs. Galloway."

Jean LaBerge could see Mrs. Galloway's chin quiver as she fought to hold back the tears. He stepped to the edge of the desk as he said, "Is there a cemetery in the settlement where we can bury Mr. Patterson?"

"Yes, there's a small cemetery on the east edge of town," said the doctor. "I'm quite sure you can bury him there if you like. I'll direct you to the man who looks after the cemetery. I think he charges ten dollars for the burial plot and will construct a simple pine coffin for twenty dollars. I believe he can also make up a wooden cross marker or even a small stone marker for you if you wish. I think he charges two dollars for a wooden marker, but I don't know what he charges for a stone marker."

Mrs. Galloway had regained some of her usual composure as she said, "Yes, we must give Mr. Patterson a Christian burial. We will go immediately to see this man who looks after the cemetery and make the necessary arrangements. Hopefully, we can bury him tomorrow."

Following the directions given by the doctor, they went immediately to the man who looked after the little cemetery and Mrs. Galloway requested that he construct a coffin and prepare a grave. She also gave him James Patterson's personal information and asked him to make up a small stone marker and place it at the head of James' grave when the marker was finished.

Their business with the funeral for James completed, LaBerge and Mrs. Galloway made their way back toward the tavern. Before they had reached the tavern, they met Keaton and Taggert returning from their quest to find a stable for their horses and a place to bed down for the night. LaBerge turned to Keaton. "Will you look after Mrs. Galloway for a half hour while Taggert and I go on to the tavern. I want to see that Calvert and his men are preparing to leave the settlement and I believe it best if Mrs. Galloway isn't present in case there should be any trouble." He paused for a moment and then continued. "I shot one of his men. If he's not able to travel, I'll allow him to remain here in the settlement. I don't want him to die because Calvert has forced him to travel."

"That's very thoughtful of you Mr. LaBerge," said Mrs. Galloway. She turned to Keaton as she said, "Let's you and I take a little walk up along the street and get acquainted." She turned to LaBerge. "We'll see you in about a half hour."

LaBerge and Taggert walked along the street back towards the tavern. He glanced up at the sky and watched the scudding clouds sail east. The rain had stopped, and he could see patches of blue breaking through the clouds. Tomorrow would be a fine day. As he walked towards the tavern, he realized that he was very tired. It seemed that he had been on the move, with little rest and sleep for days. He knew that if he were to lay down in a bed, he could sleep for a dozen hours, or more. And then his thoughts turned to the beautiful girl, Hannah, and even though he was tired and worn, he smiled to himself.

She had sent Keaton and Taggert to help him. Her actions told him much of her love and concern for him and filled his heart with a longing to take her in his arms and hold her close. If it had not been for her, and Keaton and Taggert. he might be dead now and the service at the cemetery tomorrow would be for two people instead of

169

one. The thought of her happy smile lifted his drooping shoulders as he neared the tavern.

Calvert's horse and the black horse of his companion, who had been with Mrs. Galloway in the doctor's office, stood in front of the tavern. As he ducked his head to enter the tavern, LaBerge hoped that he wasn't walking into another confrontation. He was pleased that he had asked Taggert to accompany him.

They paused just inside the tavern and looked about. Two of the men who had assaulted him from the rear of the alley sat at a table, nursing tankards of ale. The fat tavernkeeper stood near the bench. He looked at LaBerge with a surprised look on his face as he nodded toward the side door.

LaBerge spoke softly to Taggert. "I suggest you order a bottle of ale and find a table where you can see those two men while I check out what's going on in the back room. You can keep an eye on those two men and make sure they don't stir up any trouble." Without a glance at the two men at the table LaBerge strode across the room and pushed the door open. Calvert and the man in black stood at the side of a small bed looking down on the man LaBerge had shot. Calvert's face immediately filled with rage as he yelled. "What do you want? We can't leave because you shot this man!"

LaBerge ignored this outburst as he walked across the room to the bed and looked down at the man. The man's shirt had been removed and he could see a large blotch of blood across his upper right shoulder. The man looked up at LaBerge with pain filled eyes but said nothing.

Laberge turned to Calvert. "He needs a doctor to look at his wound. Have you sent for the doctor?"

"No, doctors cost money and . . ."

"I'm going to go and bring the doctor here. I'll pay his fee. I'll be back within a few minutes."

As he turned toward the door Calvert sputtered, "But . . . but it was you who shot him! I don't understand . . .!"

LaBerge looked back at Calvert from the door of the little room. "No Calvert, I'm sure you don't understand. You're a self-centered, money-grubbing man, who thinks only of himself. Yes, I shot this man in self-defense, but I don't want to see him die. I'm going to get a doctor to examine his wound. Don't interfere with me!" He paused for a moment and then said, "But you, Calvert, are the one who is actually to blame for the shooting of this man. There would have been no confrontation and no need to shoot this man if you hadn't abducted Mrs. Galloway." He turned and strode through the door and then out of the tavern.

Calvert stepped to the door of the small room and watched LaBerge's back as he walked across the tavern and out the front door. This was nuts; *What kind of a man was this, Jean LaBerge? Fetching the doctor for a man he had just shot!*

Fifteen minutes later LaBerge, the doctor, his female assistant, Keaton, and Mrs. Galloway all walked into the tavern. LaBerge directed Mrs. Galloway, Keaton and Taggert to a table on the far side of the room away from the table occupied by Calvert's two companions, and he and the doctor, and assistant, entered the small side room where the wounded man lay. Calvert and his companion said nothing as they retreated to stand near the wall and stood in silence as the doctor examined the man. Within a few minutes the doctor looked up and said, "Someone needs to bring me a pot of hot water. The rest of you clear out."

"I'll get the water," said Laberge as he headed for the door. Calvert and his dark clad companion said nothing as they quickly made their way out of the room and joined their ale drinking friends at the table.

At LaBerge's request the fat tavern keeper quickly went about heating a pot of water on the wood burning stove. He turned to LaBerge. "It'll take about ten minutes; I'll take it in to the doc when it's hot."

"Thanks, I'll appreciate it," exclaimed LaBerge.

The fat man suddenly reached across the bench and gripped LaBerge's arm as he said in a low voice, his face filled with wonder and question. "Why ya doin' this mister? Fetchin' the doc to fix up the man ya just shot. It doesn't make sense! Calvert recognized ya when ya first came into the tavern and his men were out ta kill ya when they left here an hour ago. I heard some of what they said and could see that they were a plottin' to set a trap for ya. I'd have liked to have warned ya but there was nothin' I could do."

The tavern keeper grinned across the counter at LaBerge as he continued, "I don't know how ya done it mister, five ag'in one, but ya sent em runnin' with their tails between their legs, Ha! Ha!"

"Well, I had some help from two men who came to my assistance. I'm obliged for their help."

LaBerge fell silent for a moment and when he looked up and spoke, his voice was soft but firm as he said, "I saw enough killing during the war and that man doesn't deserve to die. Calvert was just using him. I don't want him dead on my account."

LaBerge said nothing more as he turned and strode across the room to join Keaton, Taggert, and Mrs. Galloway at their table. He took a chair, pushed it up against the wall, leaned his head back, let out a long sigh, and slowly closed his eyes.

Mrs. Galloway said nothing as she watched this tall stranger who had come suddenly into her life only a few days ago. As she watched his shoulders relax and his breathing become easier, she mused to herself; *What kind of a man was this, Jean LaBerge? He had rescued the girl who had been kidnapped. and had come to rescue her, and he was now showing concern for a man he had shot in self-defense.*

The multiple events of the past few days had all come about because of a chance meeting with this man, when he had just happened to be passing close by when the two men had attempted to rob her and James. The stranger had immediately and fearlessly come to her aid, even though he didn't know her. Suppose this tall stranger had not been passing close by at that moment? What would have been the outcome of the encounter with the two men who were intent on robbing her and James, or possibly killing them? Perhaps she would be dead or the prisoner of those two men. Because of the intervention of this man the two men were now serving time at hard labor. And how would her controversy with Swingate Calvert have gone for her, were it not for the intervention of this man? She shuddered to think on the possibilities. None of which were pleasing.

She smiled to herself as she looked at him, obviously a very tired man, asleep with his head resting against the wall. *She owed him a great deal. How could she ever repay him?* The everyday happenings of our lives seemed to hang on a slim thread of chance. The lives, happiness, and well-being of several people had been altered because of a chance meeting with this tall stranger. Significant and great matters frequently turn on small chances. In fact, much that happens in one's life rests on little more than chance and fate. She wasn't sure of the details, but she felt that the chance meeting with this stranger had altered and changed her life. She smiled again; she would probably meet the young lady that he had gone to rescue, within a few days. Where would that meeting lead her? What new pathway would now open to her and what avenues would now be closed? Chance, chance; life was made up of nothing but chance!

Nearly an hour passed and then the door to the room where the wounded man lay was thrust open and the doctor and his assistant walked out. He paused and looked about, apparently unsure of just who he should report to. Mrs. Galloway stood quickly to her feet and walked to the doctor. "How is he?" she asked.

The doctor turned to her as he said. "He'll pull through. I've removed the ball and if he is given a few weeks to recuperate then he'll mend and be as good as new."

"Good, I'm pleased to hear that he will recover." There was a commotion at her side, and she looked up to see Swingate Calvert as he looked at her and then at the doctor with hard eyes. He was about to speak, but she didn't hesitate as she turned on him and spoke in a harsh voice. "Calvert, this is all your fault!" She rose up to her full height as she shook her finger in his face, like a school mom would scold a child. "You take care of that man and see that he recovers from his wound. Don't treat him like you treated Mr. Patterson and force him to ride a horse before he is ready to ride."

The doctor spoke to Calvert. "The lady is right sir. You let him take it easy for several weeks before he gets on a horse."

"But . . . but that man, LaBerge, has ordered me to leave town today. I . . ."

LaBerge's voice rang across the small tavern. He had eased the chair forward and was leaning on the table as he spoke. "You can stay Calvert. Stay as long as you like, just don't interfere with Mrs. Galloway again!" He stood to his feet and strode across to stand at the side of the doctor. He looked into Calvert's pudgy face as he said, "Give us your word, Calvert, here in front of the doctor, that you will not make this injured man ride out of here before the doctor says it is safe for him to travel."

Calvert's eyes darted about the room for a moment and then he said, "Yeah, I give ya my word. I'll not leave with him until the doc says he can go."

"And you also give me your word that you will cease harassing Mrs. Galloway to sign the deeds. That has to be part of the deal also. Calvert."

Calvert shifted his gaze to Mrs. Galloway as he spoke, "I don't know where ya found this man, but he's beaten me. I give up. I'll not bother ya further."

Mrs. Galloway managed a smile as she glanced at LaBerge and there was a sly grin on her face as she looked up at Calvert. "It's strange Mr. Calvert, but you see I didn't find him, he found me." A broad smile filled her face now as she exclaimed, "You'll have to admit that he's quite a man. Between him and his dog, with a little help from my umbrella and his two friends, he licked all five of ya. Yes sir, he's quite a man!"

CHAPTER 23

Together Again

The burial of James Patterson, at two in the afternoon the following day, was a sad gathering of only a few individuals. The usual accruements and details befitting a funeral for a loved one and friend were conspicuous by their absence. The little cemetery had only recently been hacked out of the brush and trees of the wilderness and it appeared, stark, rough, and cheerless, even in the bright afternoon sunlight, which splashed across the little enclave. Even the usual songs of the wild birds seemed to be absent, as if they had flown to more pleasant quarters to build their nests and to scrounge for food. The freshly opened grave appeared ugly and muddy, from the frequent rains, and was a most uninviting final resting place for James Patterson.

After they had left Calvert and his men in the tavern LaBerge had asked the doctor if there was a minister in the settlement. "Yes, we have a very small congregation of worshipers who meet in homes, as a church has not yet been constructed. They had sought out this minister and he had agreed to conduct a short gravesite service for James.

LaBerge stood next to Mrs. Galloway, his hat in his hand, as he listened to the minister read a few verses from the Bible about man's life being little more than grass that comes with the spring rains, flourishes for a few fleeting weeks, and then withers, dies, and is forgotten. He had not known James Patterson well, but the words seemed so inadequate to express the details of a man's life. Surely

175

there was more than birth, a quick, short life, burial, and then you were soon forgotten. LaBerge's gaze shifted from the unpainted wooden box, which held the body of James, to the open grave where the box would soon be lowered and covered with the muddy dirt. Within a few years the box would rot away and soon there would be nothing left of James Patterson but a few bones. Within a few fleeting years only a few people would remember him and within a generation or two all memory of him would be lost to the ravages of time. The admonitions of his mother, when he was leaving to join the militia, came back to him: *Jean, Jesus promised that his Father was preparing homes in Heaven for all those who accept Christ's offer of redemption and forgiveness. Christ has promised to return and gather these people, both the living and the dead, when He returns. You need to always be ready to meet Christ when that great day arrives.*

He had faced death often during the long struggle for independence. Most, especially the young, took life for granted, but he had learned that death could come in an instant, and when least expected. He had survived the war and his journey, thus far, to the far wilderness, but was he really ready to meet Christ when he returned. It was a sobering thought, and as he stood beside Mrs. Galloway, his hat in his hand, the lithe man from Vermont bowed his head and prayed that he would be ready when that great day came.

LaBerge instinctively placed his arm around Mrs. Galloway as she sobbed softly to herself as the minister brought his remarks to a close with a short prayer admonishing the Lord to accept the soul of this man and to comfort his loved ones. Laberge knew nothing of James Patterson's past and family. He assumed that Mrs. Galloway would communicate with his family if he had any.

With sparce conversation they made their way from the wilderness cemetery and back to the tavern. At the tavern Mrs. Galloway excused herself and said that she intended to retire to her room and rest. LaBerge stepped to the door leading to the side room where the man he had shot lay. He found the man propped up with a couple of pillows under his head and staring up at the ceiling. LaBerge walked to the bed and looked down at the man. "Are you feeling better?" he asked.

"Yes, much better," he responded in a hoarse voice.

LaBerge glanced about the small room, "Where's Calvert?" he asked.

"I've not seen him since shortly after you left yesterday." A faint smile on his face. "My guess is that he's skipped out and left me." He lifted his head up slightly from the pillow, "Calvert cares nothing about me; he cares only for himself and for money. I think he's abandoned me." His head fell back against the pillow. "I was a fool to take up with the man. I'm not sure what I'm gonna do when I get out of here. I'm near dead broke."

LaBerge stepped to a small desk that sat against the wall of the room. He pulled drawers open until he found a scrap of paper and a pencil. He bent over the desk and spent several minutes drawing out a rough map and then walked back to the bed. He handed the paper to the man as he said, "I'm leaving here for a place called Blue Valley in the newly opened Ohio Territory. This sketch shows you how to get there. When you're able to travel come and find me. I'll see that you find work, and a place to live." LaBerge reached for his money bag and took out a generous number of coins and placed them on the bed beside the man. "Here's some money to tide you along. I'm going to see the doctor and take care of his charges." He patted the man on the shoulder. "Take care of yourself and be sure and look me up in Blue Valley."

The man looked up at LaBerge with eyes that were filled with wonder and gratitude. "Why are you doing this for me. I . . . I have done nothing to deserve it. In fact, I was trying to harm you when you shot me in self-defense."

LaBerge smiled down at the man. "You need a break and a change," he said, "And besides, there is something in the Good Book that says you should do unto others as you would have them do to unto you."

*****

It seemed to Hanna Cody that Jean LaBerge had been gone forever in his quest to rescue Mrs. Galloway, even though, in reality, it had been only a few days. In fact, her anxiety had been so great, from the very moment he had left, that she had gone to Keaton and Taggert and induced them to leave immediately and attempt to overtake him and then lend him whatever assistance he needed to rescue Mrs. Galloway. "He'll most likely be outnumbered and in grave danger," she had cried. "Please go and help him!"

Fortunately, the two men had readily agreed and had left within a couple of hours. She hoped they had been successful in finding LaBerge and in giving him whatever assistance he would need.

Notwithstanding the willingness of Keaton and Taggert to go and help LaBerge, by the end of the third day her anxiety had risen to a fever pitch and her worry and concern had compelled her to begin a daily vigil at a shady spot that overlooked the trail of his most likely return. She was drawn daily to this overlook by some mysterious and compelling force that was new to her, and which stirred her heart in concern and fear for this tall man from Vermont. She usually came to this observation spot as soon as she had completed her morning breakfast, and scarcely left during the entire day.

Her father frequently came and sat with her for an hour or two and he sometimes entreated her to give up her watch and return to the inn with him. "Your vigil here will not bring him back one minute sooner," he would exclaim with a loving and patient face.

"I ---- I suppose you are right," she would respond with a sad and troubled look. "But it gives me hope and comfort to wait here for him." Her eyes had brightened as she continued, "I'll be able to see him from some distance when he does return. When I see him, I'm going to go to meet him. I'm sure he will like that."

If her father persisted with his entreaties, she sometimes heeded his call to leave for a few hours, but her heart continued to be filled with foreboding and concern for his safety. *Suppose he never returned?* The very thought of it was unbearable and would sink her into further despair and despondency.

Fortunately, the rains had passed, and the days were filled with sun and fluffy white clouds that sailed across the deep blue sky, as she sat in the shade, waiting and watching for him to return. Her companions during this vigil were the songbirds that flitted from tree to tree and sang melodious songs to her, and the squirrels who sniffed about her feet as they looked for a handout of food. She had found a small book, a novel, at the tavern and she read from this book as the hours passed, glancing up every few moments to look along the trail, hoping to see him. The book was a love story about a young man and woman who had found each other shortly after a settlement had been established in what would become Boston, Massachusetts. Over a hundred and fifty years had passed, and many things had changed since then, but she readily understood the trials and tribulations that came to this young couple as they overcame the obstacles to their love for each other.

She usually brought a sandwich along to eat during her daily watch and she was munching on the sandwich, when, from the corner of her eye, she caught a movement far back along the trail as something moved through the trees. She didn't immediately jump to her feet as she had frequently seen deer or elk, and once a bear, moving along the trail and the edge of the trees. Whatever she had seen was lost from her sight for several moments and then suddenly she saw a horse and rider and then another horse and rider. The sandwich fell from her hand as she jumped to her feet. It was him! It was Jean LaBerge and the woman he had gone to rescue. Oh, he had returned! She was on the path in a moment and running as she called out, "Jean --- Jean, it's me, Hannah. Oh Jean, you've come back!"

She could see them clearly now, and then he saw her and dug his heels into his horse's flanks and began to gallop toward her. His face was filled with a broad smile of surprise and happiness as he pulled his horse to a halt and jumped from the saddle. He swept her into his arms as he exclaimed. "Oh, Hannah, you were watching for me. I've come back, Hannah, just as I said I would!"

Mrs. Galloway stopped her horse and watched the young couple as they embraced. She mused to herself: *They are obviously in love. I wonder when they plan to marry.*

CHAPTER 24

The Wedding

L aBerge lifted Hannah up into the saddle and then swung up behind her. His strong arms encircled and comforted her with an assurance of protection and love as they rode into the small settlement. With peace and contentment in her heart she relaxed and leaned back into his arms. It was her fervent hope that they would never be separated again.

Jedidiah and Cathedra Cody greeted them as they dismounted at the tavern, and both could not help but note the sparkle and excitement in their daughter's eyes and face. They had no doubt; Jean LaBerge would be their new son-in-law within a short while, and they were both very pleased at this happy prospect. They both greeted him with heartfelt affection and expressed their pleasure at meeting Mrs. Galloway.

The day was sunny and warm, and they found rough chairs along the porch that fronted the tavern and at the urging of Cody, LaBerge related the details of the rescue of Mrs. Galloway, including the timely arrival of Taggert and Keaton, and the death and burial of James Patterson. LaBerge concluded his brief narration as he said, "I'm of the opinion that we have seen the last of Swingate Calvert. He apparently pulled out during the night and even left one of his wounded men behind."

At the mention of the wounded man Mrs. Galloway immediately related how LaBerge had shot the man in self-defense and how he had subsequently sought medical attention for him, had paid for his care, given him money, and invited him to come to Blue Valley where he would find work for him.

Mrs. Galloway paused for a moment as she looked along the porch at Hannah, who was seated next to LaBerge, as she said, "Young lady, I hope that you appreciate this man I believe you are going to marry. He is a man of great integrity and courage. You are very lucky to have found him. If I were a generation younger, I'd give you a run for the money for him, but I'm too old and so he is yours." She paused as she smiled at Hannah. "But I can readily see that you are also a young lady of refinement and integrity. The two of you will make a fine couple and I predict you will raise a right nice brood of children."

As Mrs. Galloway was completing her admonitions to Hannah, a horseman rode up to the front of the tavern and handed down a large bundle to LaBerge. "If ya will sir, please give this to the innkeeper. It's a package of the latest newspaper from Philadelphia. It's only three days old."

"Sure, I can do that for you," replied LaBerge. He took up the heavy bundle, entered the tavern and walked to the fat man who stood behind the counter. "Here's the newspaper from Philadelphia. I'll buy one from you. I haven't read any news in a good long while."

"Sure," said the aproned man as he cut the string and unwrapped the package. He handed LaBerge a paper. "That'll be five cents," hope ya find something of interest ta read."

LaBerge took his newspaper and returned to the porch. He settled himself back into his seat and shook the paper open. Almost immediately his eyes fell on a large caption halfway down the front page. **PENNSYLVANIA SUPREME COURT RULES TO RETURN PROPERTY CONFISCATED FROM LOYALISTS.**

LaBerge quickly scanned through the article and then handed the paper to Mrs. Galloway. His face was filled with a broad smile as he said, "Read this Ma'am. It appears that all of your property is going to be returned to you!"

Mrs. Galloway spent several minutes reading the article and when she looked up there was a broad smile across her face. "Praise the Lord! I can go home now and claim my property!" She fell silent as a cloud came across her face. "My, how I wish that James was still here to see this newspaper article and to return with me." She looked along the porch at LaBerge. "It is too dangerous for me to travel alone, and I cannot ask you to see me safely home. You have already given far too much of your time to assist this old lady. Perhaps I can ----"

"I wonder if Jake Herat would be willing to accompany you back to your home?" interrupted LaBerge.

"I would be pleased if he would agree to do so," exclaimed Mrs. Galloway.

LaBerge looked at Hannah. "Will you ride with me tomorrow to Herat's cabin and see if he will agree to accompany Mrs. Galloway to her home?"

"Yes, I'd love to go with you. I don't want to be separated from you again."

"Good, we'll leave early, shortly after we've taken breakfast."

Mrs. Galloway shifted all of her attention to Hannah and Jean LaBerge. A broad and mischievous smile filled her face as she said, "Now that I've gotten acquainted with the two of you, I'm quite certain you will be married within a few months, if not sooner. I would very much like to attend the auspicious event." Her eyes were filled with devilment as she exclaimed, "You would make this old lady happy if you would set a date for day after tomorrow for the wedding. Would you do that for this old Loyalist?"

LaBerge's eyes settled on Hannah's beaming face as he said, "How about it, Hannah? I've already asked you to marry me, and you have accepted. We just haven't set the date yet. How about day after tomorrow?"

Her face was filled with a huge smile as she looked up at him. "Jean LaBerge, I'm willing to marry you here and now, on this front porch!"

Jean turned to Mrs. Galloway. "It's a deal, we wouldn't want you to miss our wedding."

LaBerge turned to Jedidiah Cody, a broad smile on his face as he said, "Sir, if you give your consent, I will marry your daughter day after tomorrow."

Cody jumped to his feet, walked forward and placed his hand on LaBerge's shoulder as he exclaimed. "Nothing would make me happier. You have the wholehearted consent of both my wife and I."

Within a few hours the news of the pending wedding had spread throughout the little settlement like a wildfire through dry grass. After all, this was a frontier settlement and weddings were a rare occurrence. No announcements or invitations were sent out however, the people of the community were intrigued by the stories and rumors that swept through the community of how the tall handsome groom had rescued the beautiful bride when she had been kidnaped. And their interest was further enhanced when they learned of his rescue of the Loyalist, Mrs. Grace Galloway. These were not everyday occurrences, and it set the small community abuzz with talk, gossip, and speculation, especially about the tall stranger and the beautiful young lady, who had suddenly come into their midst. Never mind that they did not receive formal invitations to the wedding. They planned to attend this singular event.

Several women came forward with nearly complete wedding trousseau's that they had hastily retrieved from trunks and shelves. These were presented to the bride-to-be with the admonition, "Please feel free to use these Ma'am!" Others went swiftly about the task of preparing a cake and refreshments for a reception following the wedding. Upon inquiry by Jean LaBerge the bride and groom were directed to a man who held himself out as a preacher, although his church was yet to be constructed. "I would be most honored to perform the ceremony," he had exclaimed.

And so, the tall stranger, Jean LaBerge and the beautiful Hannah Cody were joined together in holy matrimony to the smiles and cheers of the people of the small settlement of Williamson, Kentucky. Everyone was of one accord; they were a perfect couple, and many happy years of marriage were sure to follow.

CHAPTER 25

The Parting

Two days after the wedding the newlyweds, her parents, and Mrs. Galloway and the hermit, Jake Herat, left the settlement of Williamson and rode north along the Big Sandy River toward Huntington, on the Ohio River, where they would part company. They did not attempt to travel with any haste, as they were leading three heavily laden pack mules and LaBerge's burro. They made camp the first night on the edge of a green meadow that abutted the small river. The men rustled up firewood and built a roaring fire and the three women made up a tasty batch of venison strew and biscuits from the supplies they had packed onto the mules.

Fortunately, the sky remained clear, with no rain clouds in sight, and the temperature mild and comfortable. LaBerge and Cody laid out the bedding for each party, taking particular interest to assure some modicum of privacy for each separate party, but especially for Mrs. Galloway.

Following a breakfast of hotcakes, they stowed their gear back onto the mules and continued their journey north along the river. The ride was pleasant and full of friendly conversation, and they arrived in the settlement of Louisa well before sundown. LaBerge led them to the tavern and sought rooms. "I've only got two rooms," exclaimed the fat tavern keeper. "Sorry about that."

"We'll take the two rooms for Mrs. Galloway and Mr. and Mrs. Cody," said LaBerge. The rest of us will find other accommodations. He turned to his bride of two days and the hermit. "There is a small stable up the street. We'll stable the animals there and I'm sure the owner will let us sleep on some straw."

Hannah smiled at her new husband. "I doubt there will even be a stable when we reach Blue Valley. Sleeping on straw with you will be just fine. I'll snuggle close to keep warm."

The hermit laughed as he said, "That will be fine LaBerge, except I don't have anyone to snuggle up to. Ha! Ha!"

LaBerge had a sly smile on his face as he replied, "You should give up this life of a hermit and find a lady to marry. Perhaps Mrs. Galloway can introduce you to a likely prospect that she may know who lives in her hometown."

The hermit laughed again. "Yeah, I may just do that, especially if she's as pretty as your Hannah, Ha! Ha!"

LaBerge turned back to the tavern keeper. "Have you seen anything of Swingate Calvert since he left in the dark of the night a few days ago?"

"Nope. He seems to have vanished. I think yer dog put an almighty fear into the man. I don't think he want's anything more to do with ya!"

"Good," exclaimed LaBerge. He turned to Herat. "When you head east with Mrs. Galloway keep an eye out for this man. I suspect that he knows the "game is up" for him, now that Mrs. Galloway's property is going to be returned to her, but it won't hurt to keep your guard up."

"No problem," smiled the hermit. "I'll handle him if he shows himself, even without the help of your dog."

LaBerge turned back to the fat man. "How's the man that I shot?" Is he making good progress?"

"I've moved him to a small shack I have out back. He's doin' better every day. He's there now."

LaBerge turned to Herat. "If you will take the animals on to the stable, Hannah and I will look in on this man and see how he's doing."

"Take yer time," said Herat. "I'll take care of the animals and make arrangements for us to bed down at the stable."

They found the man LaBerge had shot propped up against a pillow on a small cot, a book in his hands. He laid the book down onto the bed and his face was filled with surprise as he looked up at LaBerge. "I didn't expect to see you again for some time," he exclaimed. "Least ways not until I followed the map ya gave me to this place you call Blue Valley."

His eyes fell on Hannah. "Who's the young lady?"

"This is my wife, Hannah. We were married just a few days ago."

The man grinned at LaBerge and Hannah. "It appears to me that ya both done right well for yourselves."

Hannah stepped forward and held out her hand. "I'm pleased to meet you sir. Have you a name?"

"Yeah, sure. The handles Rags Calhoun." He laughed softly. "Kind of a crazy name, *Rags.*" But then, most everything about me has been mixed up and a little crazy."

"Is the doctor taking good care of you Rags?" asked LaBerge.

"Yeah, he says I'm doin' fine. He comes by and looks in on me every day and says I'll be able to travel in three or four weeks, but not to rush things."

"You stay here until the doc says it's okay for you to travel and then you follow the map that I gave you to Blue Valley." LaBerge smiled down at Rags. "It'll be a new start for you, Rags. A new start in a new settlement in the Ohio Wilderness, where a man can own a piece of this great land and build something for his very own."

Rags Calhoun looked up at LaBerge and Hannah, his voice cracked with emotion as he said, "You folks have been awfully nice to me. It's a good deal more than I deserve."

"I have an ulterior motive," smiled LaBerge, "We're going to be opening up a new settlement and I'll need all the help I can get. I'll see to it that you are paid a fair wage and that you get a plot of land. In addition, I'll help you build a cabin and who knows, there might even be a young lady there who will take an interest in you."

"Yeah, it would be great to have a piece of land I could call my own. I've never had anything like that before where I can settle down and stop this wondering about and taking up with the folks like Calvert." Rags grinned up at LaBerge. "I don't know about a wife! Not sure any woman would take a likin' to me, but it *would* be nice." He glanced at Hannah. "I'd feel as if I went to Heaven if I could find a woman like this here gal ya just married. Man, that *would* be nice!"

"That's impossible," exclaimed LaBerge as he smiled at Hannah. "She's one of a kind. They broke the mold after they made her."

"Yeah, ya may be right," sighed Rags. "But, no matter, I don't have any money to support a woman!"

LaBerge's voice took on a serious tone as he said, "Speaking of money, how you fixed to pay for your meals and to make your way to Blue Valley."

Rags said nothing as LaBerge took out his leather pouch and dug out some coins. "Here is a little more to make sure you don't run short before you get to Blue Valley."

"Thanks man," exclaimed Rags. "I could have probably made it on what ya gave me before."

"I don't want you to run short," replied LaBerge. "We hope to see you in Blue Valley in a few weeks."

Rags reached and grasped LaBerge's arm. "Yer a good man, Mr. LaBerge. I'll be there as soon as I can travel."

Hannah and LaBerge stepped from the shack and stopped between the shack and the rear of the tavern. They stood very close as they looked up at the sky and watched a few soft clouds scudding slowly across the azure blue sky. Hannah gripped his arm as she turned to face him. She looked up into his eyes as she said, "Jean LaBerge, I see that in addition to marrying a handsome, courageous, and resolute man, I have also married a man of forgiveness, compassion, and generosity." She quickly rose on her tiptoes and kissed his lips. "I'm so lucky and happy that you were there on the flatboat that day in Pittsburg to help my father get the oxen and wagon on board."

She stepped away and smiled up at him. "It's strange and sobering when you think on the things that determine the path of your life." She fell silent for a long moment as she looked up at the sky and then she turned back to LaBerge. "It seems that life is little more than a game of chance. We met there on the flatboat just by happenstance. You could have been there to board a day earlier, or we could have arrived a day later, and . . . and we would never have met." She rose on her toes again and kissed him. "Have you thought of that Jean? Oh Jean, it seems as if so-much of what happens in our lives hangs on the slender thread of chance meetings and happenings. I'm so thankful that the god of chance brought us together!"

LaBerge smiled down at his bride, as a look of wonder and love filled his face. He said nothing in reply to her observations for a long moment and then he said, "Yes, our lives, and all that follows, often turns on what usually appear to be insignificant moments and events, and yet their portend can be huge and can change the very course of our lives."

She squeezed his arm as she looked up at him. "Meeting you that morning on the flatboat has certainly changed my life, and all for the better." She giggled as she continued, "I was excited to be coming west to the frontier but was concerned if I would find a man to my liking, that I could take for a husband, but I no longer have that concern. I've found and married the most wonderful man in the world!"

He smiled down at her. "I'm not sure about that, but I'll try my best."

Early lamp light threw yellow patches from a tavern window upon the dust of the yard behind the tavern, and a flight of sparrows chirped loudly from an old tree that shaded the shack, as the couple kissed and clung to each other for a long moment and then they returned to the tavern and their friends.

They took their evening meal at the tavern, stretching the meal out as they visited and laughed. It would be their last meal together. Mrs. Galloway and the hermit, Jake Herat would leave for her home in Pennsylvania tomorrow.

Without preliminary, Mrs. Galloway turned and looked across at Jake Herat for a long moment, a crooked smile filled her face as she said, "Mr. Herat, you are making a big mistake living the life of a hermit and eschewing the taking of a wife. I dare say, the day will come when you'll wish you had a wife and some children. Mark my words!" She fell silent for a moment as she smiled at him. "In fact, I know a young lady, that I believe would make you a fine wife, who would keep you on the straight and narrow pathway. When we get to my home, I'll discuss the matter with her, and if she is interested, I'll introduce her to you. Don't you run her off! You'd be a fool to do so."

These admonitions from Mrs. Galloway left the hermit at a loss for words, but as he looked across the table at LaBerge and his bride, unexpected and hitherto unknown feelings began to stir in his heart. Perhaps a woman in the cabin wouldn't be a bad idea. She could do the cooking and cleaning. And he did have to admit that it would be nice to have someone to talk to once in a while, and yes, a son would be nice. Perhaps he should reconsider his aversion to women, but he would need to be very careful. *No nagging and demanding woman! Just a good, plain, hard-working woman, who wasn't afraid to get her hands dirty. He'd have nothing to do with those delicate, helpless, or nagging types.*

There was a broad grin on his face as he said, "Thank you, Mrs. Galloway, I'd be right pleased to have you introduce me to this lady."

Promises were exchanged that they would make an effort to meet again. Mrs. Galloway was adamant as she looked across the table at LaBerge and Hannah. "We must keep in touch!" she exclaimed. She produced a paper and pencil and wrote out an address and pushed it across the table to Hannah. "Here is my address. Please write to me and tell me of all that is going on as you organize the new settlement in Blue Valley."

Mrs. Galloway laughed, with a hearty, deep throated laugh, as she continued, "And there will be children and you must write me when your children begin to arrive. I want to hear everything about them." A broad smile crept across the old lady's face as she said, "Would you be so kind as to name the first baby girl that is born after me. Will you please name her Grace? I'd like that very much and I would be pleased to be her godmother."

Hannah glanced at Jean for a moment and then she smiled across the table at Mrs. Galloway. "Oh yes, Mrs. Galloway," she exclaimed. "We would be honored to name our first daughter after you and for you to be her godmother."

Hannah looked at her new husband as she said, "Jean, we must plan on making a trip back to Pennsylvania to see Mrs. Galloway after our first daughter is born."

"Yes, we must keep in touch by writing to each other, and we will, indeed, plan on coming to visit you when our daughter is born, and she is old enough to travel. Seeing you again, with a new baby, will be very special."

The bright morning sunshine spilled down over the hills and into the valleys and along the Ohio River as Mrs. Galloway and the hermit, Jake Herat, boarded the flatboat. Laberge assisted Herat in getting the horses and pack mule aboard and properly secured. He shook hands with Herat as he said, "It's been a pleasure meeting you and I must thank you for agreeing to accompany Mrs. Galloway to her home."

"I'm pleased to see Mrs. Galloway safely returned to her home. And do stop in and see me if ya are ever passing near my cabin." He guffawed a loud and hearty laugh, "But if I should get hitched up with this gal, Mrs. Galloway is going to introduce to me, I may not be there at my old cabin. She'll likely want something a little fancier. Ha! Ha!"

"Herat, if you do give up living as a hermit and marry, give some thought to pulling up your stakes there at your cabin along Wolf Creek and coming on West with your wife to the Ohio Territory and settle in Blue Valley. You could continue to hunt and trap, and you can get in on the ground floor as we build a new settlement. You think on it." exclaimed LaBerge.

The hermit was silent for a moment as he pondered this invitation. "Yea, I'll think on it." He laughed. "Gotta find a woman first!"

Laberge went to where Mrs. Galloway stood at the railing of the flatboat. She quickly grabbed him and hugged him for a long moment as she whispered to him, "Thank you, Mr. LaBerge for all you have done for this old lady and Loyalist. I'm afraid that things would have turned out much worse for me, if not for our chance meeting." She stepped back and smiled at him. "It's strange how we meet others and how much we depend on others for our safety and wellbeing. I owe you a great deal Mr. LaBerge, but if you will name that first daughter after me, my heart will be content."

LaBerge smiled down at her as he said, "Rest assured, Ma'am, our first daughter will bear your name, and God willing, we will bring the child to your home for you to hold."

They all waved to each other as the flatboat eased away from the wharf and out into the river on its journey to Pittsburg. As the boat moved out into the broad stream of the Ohio River LaBerge detected the mist of a tear in Hannah's eyes as she waved vigorously at Mrs. Galloway and Herat. LaBerge encircled her shoulder with his arm, and she looked up at him with tear filled eyes as she said, "I will miss her. I've only known her for a few days, but I've grown very fond of the lady. Once we are settled, I shall plan to write to her each week."

They stood at the wharf for a few more minutes as they watched the flatboat grow smaller as it moved away upriver, and then LaBerge said, "Let's go to the general store. We need to stock up with the food and essentials we'll need to take us through to Blue Valley. I can probably keep us in meat along the way, as the wilderness is overrun with deer, elk, and turkey." He pointed down river, "That's the ferry that will take us across the river to the north bank. I checked earlier today, and it will make another crossing in a couple of hours. It's still early in the day. We'll be able to get across and travel several miles before dark."

Two hours later the ferry eased up to the north bank of the Ohio River at a rough plank wharf. LaBerge and Mr. Cody led the horses, the pack mules, and the burro from the ferry and up onto high ground and then they returned to the ferry and assisted Hannah and Mrs. Cody up the steep slope. They stood for a moment looking about at the few rough, log cabins that lay scattered at the edge of the forest. Beyond these few buildings the hills rose up like broad stairsteps of green land, glistening in the morning sun. They were now in the wild wilderness of the Ohio Territory.

They turned and watched as the ferryman pushed off and made his way slowly back across the river to the far shore.

The men helped the woman onto their horses. "Let's be on our way," LaBerge said, a ring of excitement in his voice. "Blue Valley beckons." He glanced across at Hannah as he said, "I've been delayed and the surveyors and some of the other settlers are likely already there."

CHAPTER 26

Blue Valley

A soft breeze swept over the crest of the mountains and flowed down across the tree clad hills and into the spacious green valleys of the Ohio Wilderness. The gentle zephyr tugged at Hannah's bonnet and fluttered through the dark curls that dangled on her shoulders. The newlyweds, Jean and Hannah LaBerge, rode side by side, broad smiles of love and happiness spread across their faces, and their legs bumping each other from time to time as they talked and laughed. LaBerge's pack burro plodded along stoically behind them, while his dog, Shag, roamed about, sometimes to one side and then to the other, as he explored this new trail for rabbits, squirrels, and any other animal he could scare up. Mr. and Mrs. Cody rode a short distance back, followed by their two pack mules. Jedidiah smiled at his wife as he said with a chuckle in his voice, "Well, their courtship was fast and short, but I'm pleased. I believe our daughter has married a fine man."

"Yes, it moved along fast, with little courtship," exclaimed Mrs. Cody. "But he risked his life to rescue Hannah, and you and me, and did the same for Mrs. Galloway. He is an unusual man of courage and integrity, and I'm of the opinion that he will make a fine husband for our daughter."

They rode in a northwesterly direction, through heavily forested, rolling hills and small mountains, as they followed a narrow, hardly discernable trail. When they rode around a bend in the trail, they frequently startled a deer or an elk, that watched them approach for a few moments and would then bound into the safety of the trees. As they passed along the trail, quail and doves rose out of the brush and shrubs in large coveys and wild turkey scrambled for safety.

Hannah turned to her husband of only a few days. "We haven't seen but a few cabins since leaving the river and it looks awfully wild. Are there any Indians about? Will they attack us?

LaBerge smiled at his bride. "There are a few Shawnee and Iroquois Indians still living in the area however, following the end of the French and Indian War thirty years ago, most of the Indians moved on further west. I doubt if we will see many Indians, but if we do I expect they will be friendly. I'm told that a few Indians live on or near the land that has been awarded to me. If so, I intend to leave them be or buy them out at a fair price. I'll do anything that's reasonable to avoid a fight with the Indians.

Hannah's voice was filled with pathos as she said, "I'm glad to hear you say you wish to live in peace with the Indians. I feel sorry for them. They were here first, and we keep pushing them from their land."

"Yes, in some respects we are taking their land, but what is happening is the age-old clash of two cultures. The Indians have mostly a hunter-gather culture that has not yet come to where they embrace the concept of private property, where an Indian and his family settles down on their own particular piece of property and farm, raise cattle, or operates a business that manufactures products for sale. The Indians have been here for several thousand years, but little has changed over those many years. They have never discovered the art of mining iron ore and smelting it into iron and steel, something the Philistines did thousands of years ago to build their chariots of iron. Imagine how hard it is to cook without pots and pans! What is happening to the Indian is sad in many respects but holding back the settlement of the west is like trying to hold back the incoming tide. However, we should make every effort to treat the Indians with compassion and understanding. I'm unsure what all that entails, but a reasonable effort to treat them fairly should be made by the incoming settlers, and that's what I intend to do."

The LaBerge's and the Cody's paused briefly for a lunch of sandwiches at a small stream and then resumed their journey through the wilderness. The sun drifted slowly to the west until it hung, a giant red ball, just above the distant, haze shrouded, blue mountains. The travelers each cast long shadows when they came to a small meadow and stream. LaBerge reined in his horse as he said, "This looks like a nice spot. We'll camp here for the night."

LaBerge and Mr. Cody turned the animals out to graze on the lush grass that grew across the meadow and the two men then went about the task of preparing a small rock fireplace and soon had a fire going. Hannah and her mother prepared the evening meal while the men pulled up several logs and arranged them near the fire for them to sit on while eating. The sun was slipping behind the western skyline as they took seats and ate their evening meal.

Darkness came quickly to the wilderness, enveloping the campsite in a heavy shroud of twilight. They ate their meal in the light of the fire and welcomed its warmth against the evening chill. Immediately upon cleaning his plate, LaBerge left the fire and brought the horses, mules and burro in and tethered them near to the fire. They hadn't seen a bear, but LaBerge assumed there were bears in the area. If a bear were drawn to the area by the smell of food, it would likely spook the horses, or worse.

LaBerge threw more wood onto the fire, and it blazed high against the encroaching darkness. He assisted Hannah in washing the tins and cups and they then returned to the logs and took seats near the fire. Hannah pulled her shawl close about her shoulders against a chill breeze that swept across the meadow. Their sparce conversation was broken by the sounds of the night that came to them from the trees and brush that bordered the meadow. The yapping of coyotes and the howl of wolves broke the earie silence of the night, and an owl hooted from a nearby tree. A half-moon slipped slowly above the eastern hills and made a feeble effort to dispel the heavy gloom of the darkness. Once, when they heard nearby sounds, and stared out into the darkness, they could see the red, beady eyes of several wild animals that lurked just outside their campsite.

Hannah scooted closer to LaBerge as she said, with a shudder in her voice, "It's a little scary here in the wilderness. I can better understand the old stories of goblins and witches in the forest."

As they prepared to retire LaBerge built up a large fire and stacked wood nearby to keep it going through the night. He didn't want any of those beady eyed animals becoming so bold as to come into their camp. They were tired and retired early and it seemed to Hannah, who lay in her husbands' arms, that the sun was rising to a new day within moments of shutting her eyes.

When their breakfast was finished, they cleaned up the utensils, loaded the animals, and then pushed on to the northwest. Late in the afternoon they rode down onto the banks of a river. LaBerge consulted his crude map and announced that this was the Scioto River. "We'll camp here tonight," he announced. "Tomorrow we'll follow the river north. We should make it to my property in the Blue Valley by afternoon tomorrow."

They dismounted their animals and looked about. The land lay wild and beautiful, the river flowing past, silent and calm, its surface rippling in the evening sunlight. Off to their left, beyond the river, a valley loomed, with the dark green of the shadowed trees running up the hillsides. At the mouth of the valley, a cascade of sparkling water flowed from a small stream that tumbled down into the larger Scioto River.

As they had traveled, LaBerge had made a lucky shot with his long rifle and had killed a turkey. "We'll eat fresh turkey tonight," he had exclaimed.

LaBerge plucked and prepared the turkey. While Hannah went about roasting the meat, her mother made up a pan of biscuits and gravy. They were all hungry and the evening meal was soon consumed to the happy satisfaction of everyone. When the utensils had been washed and dried by Jean and Hannah, they all seated themselves around the fire. When the dog, Shag, had finished gulping down the leftovers he retired to the edge of the fire, curled up into a ball, and was soon asleep.

As they sat by the fire Mr. Cody turned to LaBerge. "Tell me more about the land you have been awarded and your future plans to develop this property that you call Blue Valley."

LaBerge quickly sketched out how the Ohio Company had been organized in Boston to award land to veterans of the Revolutionary War. "Those who qualify have each been awarded shares, which translate into a given number of acres per share. As a Major in the army, I have been awarded three shares, or 1,200 acres. My cost is a dollar per acre, or a twelve hundred dollars total, which is due to be paid within three years. I plan on raising the money by selling off small farms, and lots in a townsite. Since I've been delayed some in arriving at my grant, I suspect that the surveyors and perhaps a few of the people who have expressed a desire to purchase town lots or farms from me may have already arrived."

"Sounds interesting," exclaimed Jedidiah. He laughed as he glanced at his wife, and then at his daughter. "Our daughter is now your wife. The Missis and I have talked it over and we've changed our plans and will not go on to our planned destination in Kentucky. We are going to throw in our lot with you and Hannah in this new settlement in Blue Valley. I'll plan on purchasing several of the town lots from you and I intend to open up a general merchandise store." A broad grin spread across his face as he looked at his daughter. "As Mrs. Galloway noted, there will be children, our grandchildren. We'd like to be close by when they come and nearby to watch them grow up."

Hannah was all smiles as she jumped to her feet and embraced each of her parents. "Oh, Ma and Pa, that's wonderful! I was dreading the parting that would come after we took you on to Kentucky."

Mrs. Cody leaned forward and looked at LaBerge as she asked, "What are you going to name the new settlement?"

"LaBerge leaned back against a tree as he thought on her question. He smiled as he said, "I hadn't thought much on the matter of a name, but now that you make me think on it, I just may call the new town *Hannah*, in honor of my new bride." He turned and looked at her, a wide grin on his face, "What do you think? Would you like for the new settlement to be named after you?"

The flicker of the fire danced across her face as she looked at him, astonishment and disbelief filled her face, and then she sprang to her feet, stepped quickly to her husband and threw her arms around his neck. "Oh Jean!" she exclaimed, as she danced from one foot to the other. "That would be the best wedding present a girl could ask for, to have a town named after her!" She planted a hasty kiss on his lips and then stepped away, the hint of a blush on her face. "I love you, Jean LaBerge. You are the best thing that has ever happened to me. Oh yes, please name the new settlement, *Hannah*."

Their revelry, happiness, and jesting was suddenly interrupted by a low, and long growl from the dog. LaBerge turned quickly to look at the dog, who was now on his feet and staring intently into the night, his head and tail held high. LaBerge instantly placed a finger to his lips as he mouthed, "Be quiet."

They all stood in silence as they strained to look into the darkness of the night, and then the hush was broken by a high-pitched cry. Mrs. Cody's face jerked up and her eyes darted about as she whispered. "I think it's a baby crying!"

No one replied to this astonishing declaration, as silence once again claimed the forest. And then the cry came again and now it was closer. Mrs. Cody was sure now. It was the cry of a baby or a very young child. As one, they stepped toward the sound, as the dog pushed out in front of them, a low growl coming from his throat. Their fear had now been replaced with curiosity as they all moved toward the sound of the insistent cries.

Suddenly, out of the darkness, an Indian man and woman, who was carrying a small child on her hip, emerged from the forest. The man and woman stopped; their faces filled with fear as they looked at the white people. Slowly the Indian man stepped forward into the light cast by the fire as he said, with much gesturing of his hands and arms, "We see fire. Papoose very hungry. You have food?"

This statement by the Indian man caused an instant flurry of activity as Hannah and her mother quickly began to dig out the saved leftovers of the turkey and biscuits.

"LaBerge quickly stepped forward as he said to the Indian, "Yes, we have food. We can feed you and your child." He motioned for the Indian couple to come forward and take seats on the fallen logs they had been using for seats. "Please be seated near the fire. The evening is cool, and the fire will keep you warm."

Hannah quickly prepared a dish of hot turkey soup and broke a half biscuit up into small pieces and placed them in the soup to give it some substance. She gave this to the Indian woman, together with a spoon, and smiled as she watched the child take the food in hungry gulps. As they fed the child the Indian man and woman eagerly ate of the turkey and biscuits that Mrs. Cody had set before them.

Hannah turned to Jean as she whispered, "They appear to be starving. I doubt they have had anything to eat for several days. I'm glad we can help them."

"Yes, I'm glad they found us."

Hannah turned to Jean as she looked up at him in the light from the campfire. "I wonder what happened, that they are separated from their people and are wandering through the forest with their baby?"

"It's hard to say. Perhaps they can give us more information later when they have finished eating. The man appears to know some English."

Hannah moved close to her husband as she whispered, "We must not turn them back out into the night when they have finished eating. We have extra blankets. They can spend the night with us. It will be safer for them here with us." She paused as she watched the contented look on the child's face as he snuggled against his mother. Within moments his eyes had fallen shut, and he was asleep.

Hannah turned to Jean as she said, "If they have no place to go, they could travel on with us to Blue Valley tomorrow. Perhaps you could help them build a cabin and the man could work for you."

"Yes, they can spend the night with us and can go on to Blue Valley with us if they like. I sure don't want them to become hungry again."

"No, we must not send them away without food," replied Hannah. "And I hope they want to travel on with us." She looked at the sleeping child. "He's dressed in rags," she exclaimed. "I wish there were a way to get him some better clothing."

LaBerge approached the Indian couple and with hand gestures and the spoken word explained to the couple that they were welcome to spend the night with them and travel with them tomorrow. "We are traveling to a new settlement called Blue Valley. You are welcome to travel with us."

The man seemed to understand as he replied in halting English. "We stay night. Go with you when sun rise. Papoose need food." He looked up at LaBerge with pleading eyes. "You help find food?"

LaBerge smiled at the Indian man as he said, "We will help you with food. You come with us to Blue Valley, and I will see to it that you have plenty of food to eat and a place to live."

"We come," replied the Indian man.

Jedidiah and Jean dug into their mule packs and soon produced bedding for the Indian couple and the child. Laberge threw more logs onto the fire and within an hour they had all retired for the night.

LaBerge slept fitfully, as he turned over the sudden arrival of the Indian family. *What had happened to cause them to be wandering all alone in the night?*

Hannah and her mother prepared breakfast and the Indian couple and their child ate as if they were still very hungry. When they had all finished their breakfast and the plates and cups had been washed, they all moved out on their final day of travel to Blue Valley. LaBerge helped the Indian woman up onto his horse, where she rode with the child seated in front of her He led the horse as the Indian man walked beside him. Their conversation was sparce and halting, but eventually LaBerge understood that they were Shawnee Indians and that their camp had been attacked by Iroquois warriors three days ago, and he and his wife had fled into the forest with their child to avoid being killed.

"We no place to go!" muttered the Indian.

LaBerge looked at the Indian man as he said, "You stay with me. I will see that you have shelter and food if you are willing to work."

"Yes, we come with you," the Indian replied. "Must have food for papoose."

During the pause for lunch, beside a small stream and before resuming their journey, Hannah asked the Indian woman, "Can I hold the child for an hour or two while we ride? It will give you a rest for a few hours."

With some reluctance the Indian woman handed the child up to Hannah who seated the child in front of her. She spoke softly to the child and tickled its chin and the child smiled and giggled. "You're a cutie," exclaimed Hannah.

The Indian woman smiled up at Hannah and then mounted LaBerge's horse. As they resumed their journey the two women rode side by side. Hannah attempted some conversation, but the shy woman spoke little English and only nodded to Hannah's questions.

A few hours passed and then LaBerge looked back at the little party, as he said, I believe we are almost there. They all sat forward in their saddles, as they rounded a bend in the Scioto River and then they came quickly to a halt. Hannah caught her breath as she looked on the long, magnificent sweep of the valley that lay before her, green and splendid in the afternoon sun. Near the river a lone buck deer, its antlers glistening in the sun grazed. It was overpowering. It was breathtaking in its wild beauty that was almost beyond imagination and description.

Jean had stepped to the side of her horse. She looked down at him for a moment as she tore her eyes from the heavenly scene, "Oh Jean," she exclaimed. "It's wonderful! It's beautiful beyond words."

"Yes, the old trapper told me this valley was very beautiful and that's why I filed on it."

Suddenly a horse and a rider appeared from a stand of trees. He rode to the little party and then halted. "Would you be Jean LaBerge?" he enquired.

"Sure am," replied LaBerge as he held out his hand.

The man gripped his hand firmly as he said, "We've been a lookin' for you for several days. I'm running the survey crew the company sent out. We got here two days ago. We're hard at work surveying the outer boundary of your land, but we need you to tell us where you want the townsite and how you want it laid out. We'll survey in the streets and lots then." He laughed. "Of course, you will need to look things over a bit before making a decision." He laughed again as he continued, "And three of the settler families who have agreed to purchase land from you have arrived and have found land that they want to purchase from you. I guess you will need to tend to them as soon as you can speak with them and look things over."

"Yeah, I'm sorry I'm slow getting here." LaBerge laughed as he continued. "A few things came up and I was delayed."

The man looked over the small group as he said. "We thought you were traveling alone. It looks as if you have picked up some folks along the way, including some Indians?"

LaBerge laughed again as he looked at the man, a broad grin on his face. "Yes, I've picked up a few people since I left Vermont, including a wife."

The man ran his eyes up and down Hannah and there was a sly grin on his face as he exclaimed. "From what I can see, you had a right good reason for being delayed."

Hannah blushed as her husband replied, "Yes, but as you can see, she was worth the delay and the trouble."

The man pointed to a cluster of shade trees, "Some of the folks who want to purchase land from you, have set up camp among those trees. There's good water from a stream. I'd guess there's plenty of room for ya to join em. I'll let ya get settled and then we can look over yer property. I think ya will like what ya see. Looks ta me like ya got the pick of the litter; it's top-grade land, and full of deer, turkey and some bear."

LaBerge led his party to the grove of trees where they were greeted with enthusiasm by nearly a dozen men and women. They dismounted and introductions were made. "We've been a waitin' fer ya!" one of the men exclaimed, a broad grin on his whiskered face. "Tomorrow I'll show ya the land I want ta purchase from ya."

When they had set up their camp under a large oak tree LaBerge took several of the men aside and said to them. "You can see that an Indian man and woman, and their child, are with me. They are on the run from an Iroquois war party. I've invited them to settle here in the valley. If they decide to stay, I'll provide them with a cabin, some land, and employment. I'm telling you this so there will be no misunderstanding. I won't look kindly on anyone who picks a fight with them. I intend to make every reasonable effort to get along with any Indians who may be here on my property."

"Yes sir, Mr. LaBerge," replied one of the men. "We came here to farm and hunt, not fight Indians."

Laberge spent the balance of the day riding his property with the foreman of the surveying crew and keeping his eye out for the best spot for the townsite of Hannah. He was drawn to a possible site where the Scioto River made a broad sweeping turn. It was nearly level, and a small dock could be constructed to accommodate small boats.

The sun hung low above the western trees when they finished their evening meal. LaBerge and Hannah left the campsite, and the other settlers, and stole away along the edge of the stream. They walked hand in hand, saying little. They turned from the stream and walked to the summit of a grassy knoll that afforded a view back down onto the camp and along the valley.

They sat down on the grass and let their eyes take in the beauty of Blue Valley. The sun was now slipping behind the gray-green hills to the west and the scattered clouds were showing pink and red as Hannah curled her legs up under her long skirt and gave a sigh as she turned to her husband, her face filled with contentment and love. "It's so lovely. This valley will be our home, Jean. This is where we will build a log cabin and then a rambling home for our family. Within a few years we'll have a town, with stores, a school, and a church. And this is where we will raise our family and watch them grow to become adults."

She scooted to his side and let her head fall onto his shoulder for a long moment as she whispered, "I love you, Jean."

And then she lifted her head and looked at him as she said, "I'm so glad those stubborn oxen wouldn't go up the flatboat ramp there in Pittsburgh. If they had just walked up the ramp without a fuss, it's likely we would never have met."

The tall man from Vermont smiled at his bride as he said. There is a verse in the Bible that says: 'The man who finds a wife finds a good thing and obtains favor with the Lord." He drew her close as he said, "I've found a wonderful wife and I'm sure the Lord approves."

The End

205

If you would like to be notified when my next book is published, please let me know at obrown281@aol.com

AND PLEASE...

If you enjoyed this book, I'd really appreciate a review on Amazon. The number of good reviews has a direct impact on how well it sells. THANKS' MUCH

O. L. Brown is retired and lives with his wife, JoAnn, in Mesa, Arizona. His books are gentle, straight forward tales, which take the reader through a clear plot about mostly ordinary, likeable people, and their disappointments, tragedies, loves, and triumphs, to a satisfying ending, which will leave the reader pondering the vagaries of life and feeling happy and contented. His books are not about dysfunctional people, and there is no gore, sadism, or heavy language in his books.

His books are available at Amazon, Barnes & Noble, and several other online outlets. Check out his Author Page at, https://www.amazon.com/author/amazon.com.olbrown for information on all of his books.

Mr. Brown welcomes your comments and inquiries at obrown281@aol.com

Made in the USA
Coppell, TX
01 September 2023

21063496R00116